DA MAINTENANCE MAN 2

DA MAINTENANCE MAN 2

RELOADED

JOHNQUES LUPOE

DA MAINTENANCE MAN 2
RELOADED

iUniverse books may be ordered through booksellers or by contacting:

iUniverse
1663 Liberty Drive
Bloomington, IN 47403
www.iuniverse.com
844-349-9409

ISBN: 978-1-6632-3418-6 (sc)
ISBN: 978-1-6632-3419-3 (e)

Library of Congress Control Number: 2021925735

Print information available on the last page.

iUniverse rev. date: 12/29/2021

CHAPTER 1

"Wake up Quies we are here" Quies opened his eyes and slowly rased up, to see a sign that readed Foller Towne and country properties. As they drove down the road. He didn't see nothing but trees and every now and then a road that sat off to the side. He looked at Kim and asked her "where the hell she had him at. Kim smiled and told him that they were in Castle Rock Colorado.

Kim finally reached her driveway. She couldn't stop smiling. It's been years since she has been home. Pulling up to the house, Quies looked around and noticed that they were surrounded by trees. He liked that because he knew it would be hard for anybody to find him out there. Kim parked the car and everywhere got out. As they walked inside the house Kim told them to make themselves at home. Quies and Punkin walked around the house to give themselves a tour.

They couldn't believe how big this house was. Quies being to wander what her parents did for a living and what made Kim move to Atlantic. Because from the looks of it she had everything she needed or ever wanted. Quies walked around the house until he founded Kim. She was seating in the theater that was built into the house. She was on the phone crying. So he sat down next to her and wanted until she got off.

Soon as she put the phone down Quies asked what was wrong Kim told Kim how her parents was mad at her for begin pregnant and not married. Quies took her by the hand then told her not to worry about it. Cause they were married in their own little way. He grabbed Kim and told her to let him make her feel better. She started smiling as Quies begun kissing on her. Kim loved Quies because he always made her feel better no matter what.

Quies got on his knees and pulled Kim pants off, and started kissing all on her Kitty. She lends back in the seat and lifted her legs overs his head and placed them on his shoulder. Quies has begun playing inside of Kim with his tongue and stocking on her clit. The more he sucked and played, he felt himself getting hard. He unfastens his pants with one hand as he continues using the other on Kim. He slowly pulls up and grabs Kim by her hips and pulls her closer. Then he grips his dick and places it inside of her.

Taking two good strokes and Punkin came running in the room. "Quies come quick you got to see the news." He looked at Punkin and asked her was she serious as he took a few more strokes. Then he got up and ran back to the living room, to see on CNN they were talking about what he had done. They were saying it looked like a terrorist attack.

Quies had to take a seat cause he didn't know his crime scene, was gone be talked about worldwide. He couldn't stop shaking his head, he knew it was gone be a while before he could go home. But the only good thing was that they didn't say if they had a lead. Quies was pretty sure that he didn't leave any evidence behind. CNN went from talking about the case on to the killing in Baltimore. And how the protester wasn't laying down.

The world is getting tired of the law killing people and getting away with it. Quies turned off the T. V. and sat back on the sofa. Kim and Punkin sat next to him and told him that it would be ok. Instantly Quies brain went to work. He knew that he had to take care of Punkin and Kim. But he didn't know his way around

Colorado. So that was a good and bad thing for him. Then it hit him. He could become a pimp.

He seen how he had Punkin and Kim all over him and it didn't take long. Then he thought about who was he gone pimp, was it gone be Kim or Punkin or both. The more he thought about it the more he realized that it could be either. He had to find some new chicks. And what better way to get a hoe, then to use a hoe. Quies sat up and told Kim and Punkin to listen up, then told them his plan to survive in Colorado. They weren't going for it at first until Quies put his foot down.

Kim and Punkin looked at each other then said ok. Quies knew that this was gonna work out just fine. Ready to put his plan to work, he grabbed the car keys and went for the door. Punkin stopped him and told him that it was too late to be out there today. He looked at the clock and it readed 9:45 pm. Quies turned to Punkin and told her that was good timing.

"Baby just thinks about paradise maintenance service. How shun was running it" Punkin expressed

"You right baby we need to plan it out a little bit more" "Ok then we will work on it all day tomorrow but for now me and Kim got something planned for you"

Punkin took Quies by his hand and took him to the master bed room. He was looking for Kim but she wasn't in bed. Then he heard her call his name from the bathroom. Punkin led Quies to the bathroom where Kim was sitting in the hot tub. Quies took off his clothes and jumped in. Punkin took he clothes off and slowly walked over started dancing for them. Then worked her way inside the hot tub.

Kim and Punkin begin kissing on Quies. Kim took her hand

and started massaging Quies dick until he got rock hard. Then sat in his lap and grinded her way upon a nut, then got up and let Punkin have her turn. Quies wasn't focusing all he could think about was making his money. He stood up and bent Punkin over and started stroking her fast to catch his nut. Quies smacked Punkin on her ass then got out the tub.

As he walked to the bed he noticed that Kim was already sleeping. He climbed in bed next to her and lay there, until Punkin came and got next to him. Punkin laid her head on his chest while he wrapped his arms around her and Kim then fell asleep.

CHAPTER 2

The next morning Quies woke up the didn't see Punkin or Kim in the bed next to him. He got out the bed and walked through the house looking for them. They was no were to be find and Quies didn't feel like going back to the room to get his phone. Quies sat in the living room and flipped through the channel to see if they would show anything about Colorado.

But it was the same as any cable T.V. showing nothing but commercials of bullshit. Quies got up and went back to the room so he could get freshen up then find out where the hell Kim and Punkin was. 30 min later Quies got out then shower and wrapped towel around him, as he walked out the bathroom he call Punkin's phone to see where they were at.

"Baby we down stairs"

"How you know that's what I wanted"

"Cause I know you Quies, just come down here"

Quies hung up the phone and went down stairs, as he made it to the living room he saw a room full of females. Kim and Punkin rushed over to Quies and told him that this was his new stable. He just had to check out his product. But he had to put some clothes on first. Quies looked at Punkin and Kim but they wouldn't move. Quies turned around and walked back to the room, to put on some clothes. The whole time he was getting dressed he was thinking to himself. "Damn who is the pimp me or them."

But the more he thought about it, he knew that Kim and Punkin was his bottom batches. And they weren't going anywhere; they just wanted to protect what was theirs. Quies went back down stairs to the living room. As he walked around he made each female stand up and turns around in a full circle. Then picked certain one that he wanted to work the streets and the other to work only calls.

Quies knew that he could switch them out at any time. Kim and Punkin had done set him up like he had done this before. He asked all of the females how many of them have even done this line of work. But nobody said anything so Quies looked around with an angry look on face. Kim and Punkin dropped their head and walked out the room. He asked the question one more time and 3 females rasied their hands.

Quies asked them what happen to their last pimp. And they all told him the same thing, that they had done quit. Next question Quies asked them was where were they working at? And all three of them told him New York. He looked at them because he felt like they were lying to him. But he kept on moving. He knew that it was hard for a hoe to quit a pimp, so something had to happen. Quies was really ready to see what they could do and what they looked like naked.

Quies was use to seeing females naked but it all felt different and new to him. Because this time he was running shit and the females had to do whatever he said. So he made them stand up one by one and state their names then get naked.

"Hello my name is Lattrice and I'm from the south side of Colorado"

Lattrice took off her clothes and spanned around. quies looked her up and down then grabbed her on the ass and lifted her up and sat her back down. lattrice had a dark brown skin tone, short hair and nice titti with a small but fat little ass for her size. She couldn't weigh no more than 110 pounds and stood at 5'2 even. Quies took a step back and told Lattrice that her new name was La La, then moved to the next chick.

"What's up Daddy my name is shy and I'm from Florida"

Quies made her do the same thing but as she turned around, he noticed that she had a birth mark on her lower back that was shaped like a strawberry. Quies stepped back to admire shy body one last time. She stood at 5'8 with a honey brown skin tone and long silky golden brown hair with green eyes and a ass that looked perfect. Quies wanted a piece of that ass but he knew that he had to wait until the time was right.

As he moved on to the next female he just knew that he was going to get paid. Every chick in the room was a winner. From the whitest chick on to the blackest chick, Kim and Punkin really picked out some bad batches. Quies finished doing his little interview and Punkin walked back in the room and her mouth dropped. She couldn't believe that Quies had done actually made the girls get naked while he talked to them. Quies looked up at Punkin and asked her where was Kim. Punkin looked at him then replied "she's in the bed room"

Quies got up and told the ladies to get dress and grabbed Punkin by her hand as they walked off. As they made it to the bedroom, Kim was making arrangements at a free clinic for all the girls to get checked out. She told Quies and Punkin to come in and have a set. Once she hangs up the phone. She went over the plans that she had just came up with. Quies was amazed at how much thought Kim had put in to this. Kim told Quies to go get the van started up and load up the girls, while she and Punkin tied up the loose ends.

"Hold up where the hell did yall get a van at?"

"Baby I bought it today for a real good price"

"And where you get the money from?"

"Quies look around you.... You know my family got money"

"Olc smart ass, well why are we doing all this?"

"Because you wanted to and I liked the idea"

Quies walked out the room with a furies look on his face. He knew that Kim had money but he just couldn't ever put his finger on how much she had. And with her rubbing it in his face didn't make it a better. Kim made Quies feel less of a man just then but she didn't even know it. He told the girls to follow him outside to the van and to make sure they had all of their things.

Once he started up the van he walked around to the other side to let the girls in. But they had already started getting in to the van. Quies took this opportunity to show the females who was in charge. He came around the van yelling

"Ya'll hoes done lost ya'll mind, Bitch get out my damn van. I aint tell nobody to go no damn where or to do anything"

All the chicks panicked and rushed out of the van one by one." Ok now as I call out your name I want you to get in the van, "Bunny, La-La, Red, Precious, Star peaches, Strawberry, Pebbles"

As they got in the van Quies looked around to see where Punkin and Kim was but they was nowhere in sight. He walked to the front door of the house and yelled in for them to bring their ass out the house. As he turned his back to walk back to the van Kim and Punkin came out the door laughing. Quies thought to himself "Damn these two keep trying me like I aint the same nigga that I was a few days ago"

He turned around real quick and grabbed Punkin and Kim by the neck. Then gave them a look that could kill, then told them both to stop trying him. Quies let them go then walked back to the van and got in the back to set with the females. Punkin and Kim didn't know what they had done at the time but they saw and felt how serious he was. As they walked to the van the both dropped their heads trying to hide their tears.

Kim got in to the driver seat and waste no time pulling out of the driveway. As they drove down the streets of Colorado, Kim started renaissance of her pass. As she pointed out spots to Punkin whore she used to hang out at. She started realizing why she left. Kim snapped out of her little day dream from the sound of laughter.

She looked in her rearview mirror to see what was going on in the back seat. Punkin lend to the side and called Quies name to gain his attention. Quies looked up like he had just been caught stealing.

"Uhh… what's up baby?"

"We are about to arrive at the clinic"

"Oh ok that's cool"

"Umm…. Me and Kim have to show you a few things as well."

"Ok just show me when we drop the girls off"

As they drove into the parking lot Kim cleared her throat and Punkin turned back around and Kim shouted out "WE'RE HERE!" as she parked the van. Kim turned the van off and told the girls to follow her, as she took them on the inside Punkin stay in the van giving Quies the third degree. He knew that Punkin and Kim was feeling some type of way because he was back there entertaining all of those females. As he sat there and let Punkin vent he started day-dreaming about what it would be like to fuck star.

She was high yellow with reddish-brown hair and hazel and green eyes. Her ass was big enough to set a cup of water on. She didn't have no stomach and it was like she had the perfect breast, and to top it all off she was blow legit just enough to set everything off. The more Quies let his imagination run wild, he felt himself getting aroused.

"Quies are you listening to me?!"

"Yea baby I heard you"

"Why you lying Quies"

"What you mean?"

"Quies you dick is hard as a rock, I can see it coming through yo pants"

"Baby you know I like it when you be fussing at me, now come give me some sugar"

Quies you think you slick don't you"

Quies just shook his head no as he pulled Punkin closer to him. As he began to kiss on Punkin, Kim was walking towards the van. Punkin sat in his lap with her arm wrapped around Quies neck, as she looked in to his eyes and peaked his lips. Then told him how much she loved him. In the mist of Punkin telling Quies how much she loved him, Kim open up the van door? "Sorry to interrupt but here is the plan" Kim said as she climbed in the front seat and shut the door.

Kim begun to explain her ideas to them, about where she thought would be a good area for them to set up at. And as she went on with her ideas Quies started thinking to himself it Kim ever been a prostitute before. Because she had to many plans and ideas for this whole thing. He made a mental notice to ask her later. Hours had done passed and all the chicks checked out clean. That made Quies day he couldn't wait to put them to the test.

Kim showed Quies the spot as they drove by. It was a quick glance but he saw everything he needed to see. The ins and out, that was the first thing Quies always looked for. It was a old habit that he picked up from robbing. Once they made it back to the house Kim and Punkin drop off everybody and made another run. Quies start there an got to know his workers a little bit better. And the more he talks to them the freakier the conversation got. He couldn't wait to bless them with the Royal dick.

CHAPTER 3

It was show time Punkin and Kim done drop off the girls and Quies was parked on the opposite side of the street. That way he could see everything, who was coming down the streets and all of girls. He wasn't comfortable with calling them hoes yet, because he felt as if he wasn't a full pimp at the moment. He sat back and watched the girls hope in and out of cars. At this point and time he had all of them working the streets.

After the first three in a half hours Quies starte up the car and drove across the street. He collected his money and reed the girls up on comdons, as they got dropped off. Once the last girl got paid up Quies went across so he could keep an eye on things. As he sat there he began counting his money then he thought about, where in the hell was Punkin and Kim.

"Aye where the hell yall at?"

"We at the house getting things ready for the girls, for when they get back"

"Oh well somebody need to come pick up this money"

"Ok I'll send Kim and I'll finish up here"

"Okay cool"

Quies hurried and hung up the phone so he could pay more attention to the streets. He wasn't sure of what was going on with the guy that was walking down the strip with the girls. He started the car and pulled up quick

"Yo precious everything good?"

"Yeah he just wants a lil service"

"Oh okay, well gone handle that, we don't want to make a scene"

"Yes daddy"

Quies drove off smiling on the inside because he felt like he was really doing something. He drove around then parked back in his spot, and soon as he cut the car off Kim pulled VP. He signals for her to get out the van and to hop in with him. It's been a minute since Kim had some alone time with Quies she was feeling that. Quies handed her the money and told her that just the start of what's to come. Kim was thinking about the money.

She started smiling at Quies and Quies started looking crazy. He didn't know what she was up to.

"Girls what you smiling for?" what's funny?"

"Nothing baby just happy to be with your"

"Oh.... Aye check this have you ever been a prostitute"

"No! And what made you ask me that?"

"It's just how you act when it comes down to what we doing out here"

"Oh that's just because I always wanted to do this but just didn't have enough courage to do it"

"Well why when we passed by areas up here you act like you want to cry."

"Because this is my home, well ATLANTA is my home now but you know how that is"

"Yea I guess because when I was locked up I couldn't wait to get back to the city. But what made you leave?"

"Umm..... Do we really have to talk about this"

"Yea I want to know, I need to know what I'm dealing with"

"Ok here we go my dad is FBI and my mom is CIA and my ex-boyfriend was a big time dope dealer"

"See that wasn't hard"

"Yea because that's only half of it"

"Ok well finish"

Kim begins telling Quies everything that happens. And the more she told him the more he was entertain but felt sorry for her all at the same time. It was almost like dejavu with more drama cove. And in her case, her family was the folks and people were out to kill her. An as she went on about her parents, he saw she was so depressed about not being married and having a baby. Her parents were die heart Christians, they both went to college and military and now are FBI and CIA.

She was fucked, but it was nothing wrong with being a Christian or just believing in God. But she had a lot to go along with that, which made it even harder. Now it all made sense to Quies, Kim was really a rider. Quies lend over and gave Kim a hug and a little kiss on the forehead. As he wiped away her tears. He was so caught up in her that he didn't realize that the strip was full of new hoes. It was like feeak Nikk 96 Bitches everywhere.

Quies started up the car and drove over to see where all of his girls were.

"Yo red! Where are the rest of the girls?"

"I don't know daddy I just got drop back off"

"Ok well look don't get back in another car stay put and tell all the others that I'm a be right back"

"Okay daddy"

Quies drove off and went to the nearest hotel. He grabbed two rooms that was next door to each other and had a side door that connected them both. He was going to let the girls work one side while he stays at the strip. Kim was going to hold the other room down, so she could listen out for the girls. Since she wanted to be involved he had to put her in the action.

"Kim I'll be right back with the girls"

"Ok hurry back because I got something I need ask you"

"Yeah….."

Rushing back out the door Quies felt as if Kim was on some bullshit because she wanted to talk. But he couldn't let that slow him down money was starting to flow. He pulled back on the strip and saw all his hoes but one.

"Damn Bunny hasn't got back yet?"

"Yea she's over there topping some trick off" said star

"Okay well I'm about to grab the van I'll be right back"

Queis went around and went back across the street to get the van. As the girl loaded up, Quies told them to give strawberry all of the money. He wasted no time getting back to the hotel, as he pulled up his call Kim and told her to open the door. The girls got out and before strawberry got Quies grabbed her on the ass. She looked back smiling at him and slow climbed out the van and walked to the room. Quies watched that big of ass walk away in them little super girl shorts she had on.

Then ran in the room behind them and looked the doors he didn't want to get caught with his pants down. He had all of that money with nothing to put it in to cover it up.

"Okay ya'll this is where I want you to bring all of your tricks. Kim is going to be in the room right next to ya'll just in case anything goes wrong. I'm a be at the strip watching over yall there. And look always keep an eye on the car because I'm there to let your know if the cops are come and if someone trys to hurt you. Now the code for trouble coming is flashing hazard lights. Now the code for yall if you have a trick messing you or want pay, stand in the middle of the street and wave your hand. But if he is really trying to hurt you run towards the car and I'll handle the rest. But for now shower and relax until everything is done, then hit the track hard"

"Thanks cause I needed this little break, I'm tired" stated strawberry "Strawberry you take your shower first, because that comment just got you a ride back to the track with me. Anybody else?!"

"Man I wasn't......"

Before she could finish Quies was lifting her up off the bed by her neck. "Bitch you got something to say to me" Quies said as he squeezed her neck and looked her in the eyes. He dropped her and told her to hurry up. He turned around and looked at the girls and asked "Ya'll hoes want it to?" Everybody just shook their heads no, and then he walked in the room with Kim.

Kim was sitting on the bed talking to Punkin and watching T.V. But Quies didn't know who she was talking too. He gave her that look like bitch who you on the phone with. Kim just looked at him and mouthed Punkin as she continued listening to what she was telling her. It was a had to break the girls in. He knew Kim and Punkin wouldn't want that but it came along with the pimping.

"Aye I'm glad you talking to Punkin because I wanted to tell yall both that I have to break the girls in with this dick to let them know they have to do good to get it. And by doing good I mean bringing that big money in."

Kim just looked at him then told Punkin exactly what he said then busted out laughing. And continued her talk with Punkin. It was something that was said but Quies didn't question it he just walked off.

He knew that he had done got to soft on Punkin and Kim. They was getting away with to much shit. He peeked his head back in the room and told her "let's go". Strawberry had done got out the shower and was ready to go.

They made their way back to the strip, Quies jumped out and didn't even say nothing. He just went to car and got in, his mind was on how he needed get them two back in line. Strawberry walked over to the car as Kim drove off. He looked at her half naked body and told her to get in.

"Do something to make me feel good"

"Like what daddy?"

"Girl just use yo head and do something to make me feel good"

Strawberry sat there thinking to herself on what she should do, because she didn't want to do the wrong thing. That little incident back at the hotel had a little shook. But she thought about earlier when he grabbed her ass. Then reached her hand over and unzipped pants and pulled out his meat. Quies pushed the seat back then lend it back, strawberry got on her knees in the passenger and went down on him. Licking the shaft of his dick then started sucking on the head of it while she slowly jacked him off.

As she got comfortable, she went to work on him as if he was a regular trick. Quies stopped her so he could pull his pants down just enough for her to get the full size. Strawberry sucked his dick like a pro. She went from sucking and jacking to deep throating and playing with his balls. She had the sound effect and all. Her mouth was wetter than some girl's kitty cat.

Strawberry went down on him then came up and tried to give

dick head a heckie. She was sucking him so good that his toes was curling up in his shoes as he gripped the seat 15 minutes in and Quies was Cumming. Strawberry sucked real hard as he was and jacked him to make sure she got it all. Then swallowed it and smiled.

"That's for you daddy, I don't swallow for everybody"

"Damn girl I done had some mean head before but as of right now you one of the best if not the best."

"Daddy you just trying to make me feel good"

"Nah I'm dead ass, I don't cum that easy. And that's what you need to do on your tricks you can make more money that way"

"Ok I will"

"Now get out and make my money"

Strawberry didn't ask no question she did just that. And as soon as she walked across the street a trick picked her up. "Damn if she got some good head like that I know that pussy it off the chain" Quies thought to himself as he fixed his clothes. He sat the seat back right and watched all the other hoes make them. Many then beign to wonder where the hell was Kim and his hoes. He was missing out on money.

All the little dirty bag hoes was sucking up all the money. He picked up his phone and called Kim. As the voice mail came on Kim was blow the horn letting him know that they was there. Quies dropped the phone in his lap and gave Kim and the girls, the nod for them to go ahead.

"Damn this pimping shit had been in me all this time and I aint use it". Quies stated as he begin feeling his self. Kim went back to the hotel, while Quies continued doing him.

Hours later Quies felt himself falling asleep. He knew it was time to take it in; the strip had done got slow anyways. It was more of his girls out there standing around then anything. He calls Kim to come pick up the girls and they headed home. Once they got there Kim showed them were everybody was then told them goodnight. She was worn out like she had been fucking. Quies follow behind her counting money until they made it to the bedroom.

CHAPTER 4

The next morning all of the girl got up and ran to the master bed room. The door was slightly a Jared and everybody took turns peeking in. the sounds that was coming out of the room, you would think that they was watching porn. All they could see was Quies naked ass and the muscle he was using, as he pulled somebody back and forth.

He had Punkin and Kim both at the edge of the bed. Kim was laying on her back and Punkin was strawberry over her. While he hit Punkin from the back he would play inside of Kim with his finger, until he dropped down and dicked her down. he had Kim legs pinned up around Punkin like Punkin had her in the buck. But it gave him a straight shot to the pussy. As he went down on Kim to give her a little bit more before he whiched, he heard the girls at the door.

Quies turned it up an extra notch. He laid Punkin on her back and made Kim get in doggy style. Then he picked Punkin up with her legs over his shoulder then got behind Kim. He placed one leg on the edge and crossed grabbed Kim with one hand and held Punkin up with the other. While he ate punkin out, he fucked Kim from the back. Then laid Punkin back down trying not to drop her.

Then he flipped her over and slid her right next to Kim. He went back and forth, making them come back to back. It was like Kim and Punkin was wetter then they ever been. And Quies was loving it, he was not only putting on for the girls but he was paying Punkin and Kim back for all that smart mouth they been having. He pounded each stroke with extra force as he gripped that ass. Quies made them get in the 69. Punkin ate Kim while Queis hit her from the back. Kim help stimulate Punkin with her tongue.

Quies pull out and went right into Kim's mouth; she sucked and jacked him, while he played inside Punkin. He drugged them like that for a few minutes then rotated then. Quies wanted to save some excitement for the girls and to keep them guessing. So he pulled out and let Kim and Punkin take turns giving him oral until he climaxed. As he ejaculated all over their faces the bedroom door came open. Quies didn't even look back, he was to busy squeezing his checks together, while he jacked trying to get his entire nut off.

Kim and Punkin jumped and tried to cover up.

"They got the same thing ya'll got, so why ya'll covering up"

"Umm.....How have ya'll been there?" Punkin asked

"We just got here" stated pebbles

Tiffany aka pebbles was an 01 Texas girl. While with blue eyes, black hair, a typical white. But she had a little but fat booty, her pussy was big you could see it poking out through whatever she had on. And she couldn't weigh no mover then 105 pounds standing at 5'4. If you didn't no any better you would think she was a teenager but she way beyond her teens.

Quies turned around fully erected and all of the girls dropped their eyes to see his package. He saw the lust all in their faces; he just walked off like it wasn't anything new to him. As he walked inside the bath room the girls left from the bedroom door. he knew that he made an good impression because their face said it all. And that would make them work hard just to get some from their pimp.

As he showered Kim and Punkin joined him. They really wanted a round two but didn't want it to be to obvious. They loved it when

Quies dicked them down but they both noticed that he was a little rougher then ever.

Meanwhile the girls was back in the leaving room talking about what they had seen.

"I'd love to ride that dick, like I ride my horses back in Texas" giggled pebbles

"Girl you aint the only one, I love fucking a man that knows his way around the bedroom if you know what I mean" stated star.

"I'd let him hit it from the back so I could put all this ass on him just to see if he could handle it." Peaches burst out

"Well if yo head game is as good as mine, he won't be able to handle it" strawberry added.

"Girl you done experience already….. How was it?" Bonny asked

"We didn't do nothing I just gave him some head last night and its bigger and longer then you think." Stated strawberry

"When did all this happen? I had to been steep." La La commented

"While ya'll was washing up last night I left with him remember"

"Yea you did didn't you. Girl you slick I got watch you" Red said

"Girl it wasn't like that, he just wanted me to make him feel good for that moment and that's what I did" strawberry shot back at Red

"Um….. we'll while ya'll are fighting for the dick, I'm get the dick"

Precious slid her little shot in.

30 minutes later Quies came waltring in the room and the girls get quiet. "Don't get quiet now, how ya'll doing this Morning?" Quies asked,

"We good" they spoke

"Ok well this is what's going to happen today. We are going to the mall to spend a little money. I can't have ya'll out there looking like them other dirty bags."

Punkin and Kim walked down the stairs and you couldn't tell them they weren't a million dollars. Punkin was Dolce + Gabbana down with some red bottom heels and Kim was channel down to her feet. Quies knew he had two bad bitches but today they were showing off. "Now ya'll not gone come out the mall looking like them you got to put in wore before you get this type of love" stated Quies as he motioned for them to come on. They loaded up the van and headed to the mall.

45 minutes later they were at the mall and walking arounding. Kim was bumping in to people that she haven't seen in years. She was excited to see some of her old girlfriend. Quies and Punkin let her enjoy herself as they took the girls to get there gear. Quies made sure they were fly but skanky looking. He took them to get their nails and feet done. Punkin started feeling some type of way because she wasn't get the treatment, it was all about the hoes at this time Quies saw it in her eyes that she was jealous; so he set her up for a little spa treatment while he was taking care of the girls. Kim was nowhere in sight so she just missed out.

Quies had the girls passing out there cards as they walked through the mall. As they got to the food court Quies text Punkin and Kim and told them that they needed to get there ASAP. The food court was like the biggest promoting area ever. Quies sat back and watched his hoes run round handling business. All he could see was dollar signs. Kim and Punkin approached him at the same time but just from different sides.

"Look around you do you see what I see?" Quies asked

"No" Punkin replied

"What people walking around" Kim asked

"Damn ya'll smart but dumb at the same time. But the answer is money"

"Nigga who you calling dumb?" Punkin question with an attitude

"Don't start you know what I mean"

"Well I don't, me and Punkin need for you to clear that up"

Quies laughed and stood up then grabbed them both

"Ya'll know I love ya'll" Quies slide in as he signaled for the girls to come in. He grabbed all the bags off the ground and they headed out the mall. Quies was being a gentleman, he was thinking about as a pimp you make your hoes do every. As they made it to van Quies heard someone beating "switch in Lanes" by T.I. big K.R.I.T and Trevor case. He was feeling that song because it's a true statement about the government.

As they pulled out the parking lot a car cut them off, and stopped right in front o them. One dude jumped out the car and ran to the van yelling Kim's name. quies sat up and looked at her then locked at the dude.

"So it's true you are back" the guy said

"Yea I'm back but I got to go it was good seeing you"

"Girl wait to everybody else found out"

"Oh ok well just tell them I said hello" Kim said as she backed up nervously.

Quies people the move and knew something wasn't right with that nigga. But he didn't say nothing he just let her do her as he sat back.

"Aye I'm hungry what we gone eat?" Quies asked

"Oh can we get some hot wings?" asked Peaches

"Ok that sounds good to me, so we got one for hot wings anybody else"

"What about pizza?" asked Red

"Shid I like about of them so I guess that's what it is"

Kim gave Punkin the number to a hot wing spot as she called pope John's. She had the pizza delivered and they had to pick up the wings. And soon as they got to the wing spot those same niggas was up there. But this time it wasn't a happy greeting they was on some bullshit. They were calling her a rat, cop baby, and all kind of bullshit as names.

"Yo Kim do I need to handle this my way or do you got it?"

"No we good I got it; we don't need you in trouble"

"Ok well handle it"

"Ok"

Kim jumped out and grabbed the wings and ran back to the van. But before she could make it one of the guys jumped in front of her. She tried to go around him but every time she moved he moved. Quies climb over the seats and out the driver door. he grabbed the guy by the collar of his shirt and pulled him back into a hard elbow. Then pull the 40 cal off his hip and put it to his head.

"Look here bruh I don't know what you got going on but if you make her drop my food I'm gone drop you and you mans and them" Quies stated

"Man I'm sorry I was just having a little fun, she's an old friend"

"Okay that's all good but don't play with my food and if she want to kick it she'll get at you"

Quies let him up and told Kim to get in the van. He walked around the van with the pistol still aimed at the two guys. As he climbed inside he told Kim to pull off. He wasn't even in the van good enough and Kim was pulling out the parking spot. As they drove down the street Kim looked in the rear view mirror at Quies.

"Umm….. Bae that was…"

Before she could even finish Quies stopped her and told her it was no need to explain.

Quies know it had a lot to do with her pass. But what he couldn't understand was how he got stuck with two chicks that got him on the bullshit and on the run. Now he done came way up here to get away from some bullshit and damn near got put in some more. Quies didn't say nothing else the whole ride home. Once they made it back, he didn't waste any time getting inside the house to eat.

He knew that he could think better on a full stomach. 30 minutes after he was eating and had done kicked back, Quies started thinking about how he was gone get back to the city? He didn't know the ins and outs up there. Which was a good thing, because nobody knew him but it was a bad thing, because if anything was to happen it would be hard for him to get away.

"Quies baby are you alright?" asked Punkin

"Yes just thinking about my next move."

"Well since we in the room by ourselves let me help you think"

Quies started smiling because he knew were that was headed. He let Punkin. Come sit next to him on the bed. And she began rubbing on his leg and working her way up to his chest. Punkin straddled him and started kissing all on him. She lifted up the front part of her dress, so she could unbuckle his belt and unzip his pants. She pull out his softly harden penis and placed it inside of her. Grinding on him until he was fully erected.

Punkin was trying her best not to let out any noises but every time Quies hit her spot she would let out a short but sexy scream. He flipped her off of him and laid her sideways on the bed. Then grabbed two pillows, one for her to hold on to and bury her face in and the other one to lift up her ass. Quies got behind her and busted her up real good. Once he was done he laid across the bed to take a nap.

CHAPTER 5

8:00 pm that night Quies was woke up to Kim sucking his manhood. He raised up just good enough to watch her slob his meat down. He liked when Kim gave him head because she got real freaky with it. She looked up at him them said "we" finish later but for now you got work to do"

"Damn cause while you were sleeping me and Punkin had been running the girls on calls."

"What?! They been booming like that?"

Kim just smiled and threw a large stack of money at him. Quies jumped up out the bed motivated and ready to hit the track. He got dressed and went down stairs and all of his hoes was lined up. They were lined up as if they were in a molding the new gear they just got. Peaches was standing at the end of the line and her ass was hangig out the bottom of her little gold shorts. Her legs was looking extra good in them high heels.

"damn I got to tap that tonight" Quies thought to himself. But she wasn't the only one, all of his hoes was looking and smelling good. Quies open the door and let them led the way. Damn I got some bad.

ass hoes" ques thought to himself as he shook his head watching then go out the door and get in the van. As they took off, Quies drove behind them. He went straight to the hotel.

"Hello my friend I see that you are back for another night."

"Yea, I'm become a regular around her so I'm need a deal"

"Oh you must be the new pimp I been earing about."

"What?! Who told you that?"

"Now, now my friend no need to get up set, but all the pimps and hoes come here."

"Oh well yea that's me but we gone do about this room deal?"

"Well you tell me how long you want the room for and I'll give you good deal my friend."

"Okay let shoot for a month"

"Umm…Lets see…for a month, you give me $300 and let me freak two for your hoes for a week."

"That's for both rooms right?"

"Yea that's right the sane two rooms form last night."

"Ok deal but you only get to freak them once a week for an hour."

"Okay ok very good deal for me and you."

"Quies gave him the $300 dollars and told him he'd be back with the two hoes. As he climbed in the car his cell went off. "Yea what up."

"Aye do you want us to say here or meet you at the hole" Punkin asked.

"Nuh stay there I'll be there in like 3 minutes."

"Ok."

Quies hung up the phone and hauled ass down the road. He had a plan, he was going to get the two hoes that he wanted to fuck first then let Mr. Faygo have his hours with the hoes. As soon as he pull up on the strip he let Kim and Punkin, know that's where they would be at for the first half. Then went to find Peaches and strawberry. He pulled up and all the other hoes raced to the car.

"Y'all hoes get off my car I'm looking for my hoes."

"Damn nigga we didn't know you was a pimp, we thought you was a trick."

"Well hoe now you know."

As the hoes. Walked away from the car Quies scanned the area looking for strawberry and Peaches.

"You Precious where is Strawberry and Peaches?"

"Peaches just left with a trick and strawberry around the corner with a trick."

"Ok well tell all the girls that we got the same rooms from last night, then pick a girl to come with you if Strawberry is not done with her trick."

"Ok daddy I'll be right back."

As he waited for her to get back, he saw another pimp walking down the street. "Ha Look at this fool don't he know don't nobody dress like that any money. This nigga got on bright yellow suite, with a blue and white fur coat and a damn cane. Man that nigga got to be a Nugget fan with them colors on." Quies thought to himself. Precious came back and climbed inside the car.

"Are where is Strawberry?"

"She was right behind me."

"Oh there she is."

Strawberry jumped in the back seat "Hey daddy, did I do something wrong?"

"Nah just got to take care of business "Quies replied she drove off. Arriving back at the hotel Quies made them go fleshing up. Precious got out the shower with her towel wrapped around her. Quies pulled her in and took the towel from around her. Precious stood there but as naked. Precious was a white girl with a banging body. She was 5"6 with dark brown hair and eyes, a nice size C cup breast, thick thighs and with a fat ass to complete the body. If you was to look at her face you would think she was Katie Perry.

Quies had done got undress and made precious suck his manhood until he was good and ready. Then he laid her on the bed and lifted her legs up. As he inserted himself inside of her Strawberry walks into the room.

"Oh I'm sorry I didn't mean to interrupt."

"Nuh you good, I need you to come get right next to her."

As Strawberry got in bed, Quies was slowly stroking Precious. He reached over and started rubbing on Strawberry's clit getting her wet and ready. Quies pulled Precious legs up to her chest and started pumping hard and deep. Precious let out short moans as he started to go faster. She wrapped her hands around his neck and pulled him closer with catch thrust. Precious was so wet you could hear the smacking sound of each stroke.

Strawberry was beginning to get jealous and turned on all at the same time. As soon as Quies made Precious catch her first nut, he pulled out and went right inside of Strawberry. She was tight like a virgin but wetter then Niagara Falls. Quies had to re adjust himself, he took one leg and placed it on the bed as he held both of her legs up. He begun. Stroking her slowly just to get the feel of her insides. And the more he stroked the faster and harder he got.

She was screaming and moaning like someone was trying to kill her. Quies realize that she really couldn't take no dick. But that kitty was so wet he didn't want to pull out. He took a step back and told them to both get in doggy style. They both had the perfect arch in their back, and that ass spread just right. Quies jumped behind precious first because her ass was a little bit fatter. He grabbed her around the waist and pounds her from the back. Her ass clapped with each bounce against Quies's body.

Meanwhile, while Quies was handling business inside the hotel Room, Kim and Punkin was handling business on the street. They were checking out the other hoes from the van. They didn't want to get mistaking as hoes or get into it with one of the pimps. They noticed that it was only two pimps that really came out to the track. And all the hoes except for theirs and a hand full of them would go to the pimps to check in. Tricks came and went, the strip was beating tonight. And Punkin just about had idea of who she wanted to put on the team with the other hoes.

"Aye Kim do Queis story gone this long all the time?"

"Yea…Well last time I was at the hotel by myself."

"Do you think due should call?"

"Nah he's ok, well better yet let's call and tell him about.

These new hoes"

As the cell phone goes off Quies stop in middle stroke to see who's calling. "Damn she would call right when I was about to bust" Quies said as he threw the phone back on the pillow that was on the floor. He grabbed Precious and flipped her on her back and put Strawberry right next to her in doggy style. Quies wanted to make it quick so he could get the next two girls. Quies bounce and forth but he came to realize that his climax was fading away. He stopped and told Strawberry to suck him up.

He knew that was a fan show way of Cumming. Strawberry grabbed him and pulled him closer and opened her mouth wide and placed him inside of her. As she used her neck to guide her head up and down, Precious sat to the side looking crazy. Until Quies pulled out and slapped her in the mouth with him meat. Precious slowly stroked him as she worked the head of his dick. Quies shook his head because as of now he knew that two of his hoes had some good as head.

Then he grabbed Precious by the head and started jabbing her throat with his manhood. And she was taking it all, her mouth was so wet and warm it made him feel like he was fucking all over again. He let them take turn until he erupted on and in both of their mouth and faces. As he finish he heard someone come into the other room, he cracked door just a little bit to see who it was. I was Bunny and a trick, he stepped in and told her that he was next door if she needed him, and once she was due to come holla at him.

As he close the door precious and strawberry had done wiped off and was waiting for what was next. Quies call me, Faygo and told him that the girls were on their way to the front office. Once he sanded them on their way he washed off and called Punkin back.

"Yo what's good? Is everything alright at the track?"

"Yea, but me and Kim see a few chicks that don't have a pimp and they might would like to be on the team."

"Ok I'll keep it out when I get there."

Quies hung up the phone and noticed that Bunny was standing in the door way.

"What's wrong?" Quies asked with a concern voice

"Nothing, I'm done and you told me to come holla at you."

"Oh ok well it time for you to get broke in."

"Wow! I get some of that good dick daddy?"

"Yea that's right it's time to bless you my child."

"Ow daddy put it on me"

Bunny got right on her knees and serving Quies until he was all swollen. Once he was ready he picked Bunny up slowly and put himself inside of her while standing up. Bunny was built straight like a white girl. Big titts and no ass, light brown eyes and black hair and cute as a mother fucker. Quies walked around the room bouncing her up and down on his manhood. Bunny wrapped her arms around his neck and with each bounce, she squeezing kitty muscle.

Quies walked her to the bed then kid her down. As he begun to find his stroke the phone rung.

"Damn what do they want now" Quies stated as he grabbed his phone.

"Hello"

"Quies you gotta got to the track" Punkin stated

"What? I'm in the middle of something right now"

"But we need you move"

"Ok say nomo, I'm on the way"

Quies took a few more strokes then got up. Bunny laid there confused, she didn't know if he wanted to which position or if they were leaving. Quies came out the restroom and started putting on his clothes.

"Aye get dressed we will finish on another date or time.

"Ok daddy"

As Bunny got dress there was some knocking at the door. "Yeah who is it?" Quies yelled as he clutched the handle of his pistol.

"It's us daddy we're back" strawberry yelled through the door. Quies peeked out the peek whole then open the window just to make sure it wasn't a set up. As he opened strawberry and precious came in laughing.

"What's so funny and what happen to Mr. Faygo?"

"That's it daddy Mr. Faygo is so funny" Precious stated

"Well did yall handle business at least?"

"Yeah, strawberry took care of that that's why it's so funny"

"Ok well come on we got to go yall can tell me what happen in the car"

As they loaded up and drove off, Quies phone went off again. But this time he didn't even bother to answer, he just hit the gas even harder. As he pulled up on the strip his got back, things was all out of hand. It was 3 guys rocking the van from side to side. Quies parked car in the middle of the street and jumped out. As he run over to the van one of the guys popped the strap then commented "Yea who got the gun now" Quies realized off the top that it was the same niggas from earlier, but just added one.

Quies quickly backed up and got behind the car. And as soon as he grabbed his gun off his hip he heard a loud shout from the other side. "Quies! Help!"

He looked across the street and he couldn't tell if it was a pimp after one of his hoes, or if it was somebody else with these three guys. "Whatever I'ma do I need to do it fast" Quies thought to himself as he crawls back to the driver seat.

"Aye yo Precious, I need you to slide over to the driver seat and on my count pull off"

"Ok daddy but where do you want me to go?"

"Just get out the way"

As Quies explained to Precious he heard the guy voice getting closer. He looked under the car as saw him walking his was. Quies got up into a squat stands and quickly made his way around the front of the car. Then waved at Precious to pull off. As he felt the car kick out of gear, he took off running towards the van. Quies knew he was fast but not fast enough to get away from a clear shot.

But once he made it to the van and the guy didn't take his shot,

Quies knew right then those they were some studio gangsta. He tackled the guy on the passenger side to the ground, then hit him with the bott end of the pistol. Splitting his head open with the force and pressure of hitting the pavement. Quies climbed on top of the and struck him a few more times before for his friends tried to help. He rolled to the side falling off the curb in between the van, letting out two shots. Hitting one guy in the leg and the other in the arm making him drop the Beretta 9 mm

"Fuck! D-Rock that nigga shot me" Ghost shouted.

"He'll he shot cash too"

"Damn bruh I'm leaking bad, Aye yo cash you good" Ghost asked

"Yeah bruh he just hit me in the leg" Cash replied

While Ghost and his crew was trying to get back situated, Quies had jumped back in the car and head to the other side. And as soon as he crossed over he had his door open and slammed on breaks. He jumped out the car and ran over to where Red was standing.

"Yo you good?" Quies asked

"Aye but that nigga over trying to make became one of his hoes"

"Ok I got it, just tell all the girls to load up in the van we done for the night."

"Ok daddy"

Quies take off after the other pimp, and slowly creep up on him. "Aye pimping!"

"Yea! Yea! Baby what's good, you know time is money and money is time and if I spit another line it's gone cost you a pretty little dime" Pimping low rhymed

"Nigga fuck all that keep yo hands off my hoes" Quies replied as he knocked Pimpin low to the ground.

Really not having time to check Pimpin low like he wanted to, he just had to settle for that one good hit. Quies looked at the van and Punkin gave him the thumbs up, then he jumped in the car and drove off. Wasting no time to get off the scene.

"Damn daddy you don't play, you just made me wet" Bunny stated

"Girl you just a little freak" Precious laughed out

"Bitch don't be hating" Bunny shot back in giggles

Quies smiled on the inside but tried to keep a serious face. That was the second time he showed the girls that he didn't play. Quies knew that, that would have sealed their girls trust. Arriving back at the house Quies noticed that strawberry and Bunny had got real aquatic with each other in the back seat. He knew he kept hearing noises behind him but he didn't think he would see strawberry playing inside of Bunny while kissing her.

Just seeing that little bit made him want to go back to the hotel and got lose all over again. They stopped and started giggling as they got out the car. One by one th entered the house.

CHAPTER 6

An hour later it down on Quies to check and make sure all of his hoes was at the house. He climbed out of bed with Punkin and Kim and Raced to the living room.

"Everybody line up, I need to see whose missing" Quies spoke while looking around. All the girls line up at once and called out there names. "Damn where the fuck is La La at? Aint nobody seen her before we left" Quies questioned.

He looks back at Kim and Punkin then shook his head. "Yo Kim let's go find her" Quies stated as he walked towards the front door, Kim didn't ask no question she just grabbed the keys and followed him.

"Quies baby, you make a great pimp but I know you are going to be an even better father" Kim emotionally expresses

"Thanks baby but right now is not the time to be getting all soft on me"

"I'm sorry bae it's just my emotion are real strong right now"

"Don't be sorry hoe is careful!" Quies joked around

He lend over and gave Kim a kiss on the checks just to let her know thatw he was playing for real, then told her to pull over and let him out the car. "Aye go check the hotel while I walk the track" Quies shut the door and walked off. Quies made his way to the track and it was like an ghost town. It was like three hoes walking up and down track, and that was unusual for the track to be that slow. Quies searched the area as he walked but didn't see not unmarked car or even regular cop car. He just knew and felt like the cops was somewhere around. Pushing up on one of the hoes Quies asked her if she had done seen La La.

"Nah daddy but I can take care of your needs"

"Bitch you must be ready to pay me, I should make you suck this dick just for trying me. Now get out my face"

"I'm sorry daddy I didn't know you pimping; I'm not used to seeing your face around her."

"Well you better get used to it and think about joining team"

"My pimp would kill me if he found out that I was talking to another pimp, let alone leaving him"

"I'll be out here when you are ready"

Quies smacked her on the ass and walked away.

Before he could get ten feet away from her, two guys came from around the building and cop cars came down both sides of the street. Quies kept walking like aint nothing happen, the two guys told him to freeze. He looked at them and took off running. It's was really nowhere for him to go, but he wasn't just gone give in so easy. As he took off running the first thing he thought about was his pistol

Quies patted himself down just to see if he had it on him. He was so use to caring it to the point it like another piece of his clothing. Once he realized that he didn't have it on him, he speeded up. The officer jumped out of the squad car and took off behind him. Soon as he hit the corner another offices tackled him.

"Freeze do not move!" the offices yelled

"Man I aint even do nothing, why yall fucking with me?"

"Well why you take off running?"

"Because I'm black and it's two white boys coming from around building, then cop cars pull up out of nowhere and you asking me why I ran"

The officer hand cuffed Quies and placed him in the back seat of the cop car. "What's your name son?"

"Why? I aint did nothing for you to run my name"

"Well you just did and you're in a well-known prostitution area"

"Man this some bullshit! What I do and what prostitution got to do with me?"

"You'll find out when we get to the station."

"Oh hell nah yall just can't lock me up without telling me what's going on"

"Welcome to Colorado"

As the police drove down the street, Quies spotted Kim and La La going back up the road. It was like they locked because Kim hit her breaks. Quies kept looking out the back window, just to see if she was going to turn around. And sure enough she did just that. Quies phone started going off in his pocket.

15 minutes later they were arriving at the police station and Kim was right behind them. The officer took Quies inside and place him in a holding cell for booking.

"Aye yo officer don't I get one free call and can you tell me what I'm locked up for."

"Yeah we will get around to all that but your locked for soliciting for proposition and obstruction of police duties"

"Man I aint try to buy no pussy and I aint hit nobody"

"I didn't say you did" the officer said as he closed the cell door.

"Man …….. this drity ass crack just want to see me locked up"

Quies said as he aggressively punch the wall. He paste back and forth hoping that don't nothing pop up when they run his name and finger print him. Before he knew it an hour and a half had done passed, and he was getting tired. Quies laid down on the bench to relax until they called him

CHAPTER 7

"Mar-Quies white you have court in a hour"

"Damn already! I knew yall was going to try to hang a nigga"

"You got first appearance"

Quies jumped off the up bunk and got himself together. He never has been locked up in another state, so he wasn't sure how they were going to play it.

"Aye my nigga, you don't have anything to worry about."

"Damn bruh didn't mean to wake you, but what you mean I aint got nothing to worry about?"

"Man this yo first time getting locked up out here and it's for some bullshit. The judge might cut you from the court house"

"Oh yea! Man don't be acting like them jail house lawyers and don't be know what the fuck talking about half the time."

"Man I be in and out this shit for the same thing all the time and the judge fuck with me every time"

Quies and his bunkmate kicked it until the officer came back and got him. The jail and court house was in one building just like Clayton County it was all in one building. As they got to the holiday cells outside of the court room, the officer stated calling names and placing them in different holding cells. An hour or two later the officer came back to get Quies, it was like he was the first on the list as they walked into the court room Quies saw Kim and Punkin sitting on the front roll of the benches. Kim throw up her thumbs letting Quies know that she had him looking care of, but Quies he didn't know what she saying. He just thought that she was letting him know that she was there for him.

"Stated your name sir"

"Mar Quies white"

"Ok Mr. white, I see that you have a lot going on here. You were looked up for proposition soliciting and obstruction of police duties"

"Um…. Excuse may I speak?"

"Yea sure but let me remind you that anything you say can and will be used against you"

"Yeah I know…… you know what I'd just wait until my real court date"

"Are you sure it's nothing you want to say"

"Yes sir, I'm good"

"Ok well you have a bond that's already been post and we will send you your court date in the mail"

"Yes sir, so does that mean I'm free to go right"

"Yes that is correct Mr. White"

Quies was confused but happy at the same time. They handle things a lot different from Georgia. As the officer took Quies to the back they were bring the next person in. Quies was placed in a all-new holding cell. And as soon as he walked in the spotted a crowd of guys standing and sitting around one dude. He went and sat down by himself and said "Groupies" in a low tone. As time passed by niggas came an left but they all sat around that one guy.

And all he did was talk about how he was to sale dope and all the money he had. To Quies he thought that he was making himself an easy target for two things. For somebody to Robb him or for someone to testify against him. As he looked around the room again he noticed that it was only a few guys that wasn't sitting arund him.

So he didn't feel like and outside to much anymore but he knew really was. And the more that nigga ran his mouth the more he was telling on his self.

Quies feel like this was an easy come up because the nigga was giving away information. Quies slowly moved down so nobody wouldn't really notice him. he listen carefully as the nigga spoke about an operation that he still had going, and that's how he was able to still come back to fight his case. He didn't go to deep into details but if you was smart enough you could put it together. One of the guys that were standing around asked him about some girl he uses to talk to.

"Who you talking about you know I had many hoes"

"Man ice you know the white girl that you with"

"Oh you are talking about that bitch Kimberly!"

"Yeah her, is she still fucking with you?"

"Nah you know her folks had her set me up and I tried to get her done up. But they say she left town before they could clip her." Ice stated

"Man my partner told me that she was back" another guy spoke out

"Yo are you sure it was her?" Ice asked

"Yeah it was her and she was with a group of hoes and some nigga"

"Well damn that's good news I need to tell the boys it's play time"

Quies stood up and stretched then made his way in to the crowd. Everybody moved to the side to let him through but they all was looking at him funny.

"Aye my nigga watch yo mouth about my baby moma and you better stand down" Quies told Ice while he grilled him

"And nigga who you supposed to be captain save a hoe" Ice replied

"If that's what you want to call me but you need to stand down on that one"

Ice stood up as he exchanged a few more words then took off on Quies. They were having slug fest, standing toe to toe and blow for blow. Everybody crowded around rooting for Ice because that's who everybody knew. Quies knew that he wasn't going to be able to stand there any longer because Ice was every bite of 320 pounds and stood about 6'6. And you could tell that he tried to work out but no really. Quies took another good swing then backed up. But when he backed up he saw a sign of weakness. Ice was getting tired and that gased Quies up.

He went back to his old prison days and started fighting with his martial art/combat skills that he learned from John Mac and Muslim name Jalil. It was hard to fuck with him when he started up. Quies went back in and broke Ice down real quick. As he backed up he started telling Ice to stay a was from Kimberly, but before he finish everything he was trying to say all of Ice's groupies rush in on him. quies was doing his thang but it was just one to many of them.

And he wasn't trying to break any bones to lessen the number of guys, because that was a new charge and he didn't need that at the time. So he begun for fight harder and for so reason shit started to lighten up on him.

He noticed that half the crowd was in another crowd fighting with somebody else. Quies fought until those niggas started falling off. The cell door popped and officers ran in shooting pepper balls and hitting niggas with the shock shield. If you didn't get on the ground they made sure they got you there.

They placed everybody in zippy ties and one officer stood over them with the pepper ball gun and a gas mask on. The other entire officer left out and everybody else lay on floor choking and gagging. The head sheriff walked in with two photo copies and went to looking for whoever it was on that paper. He pulled out one guy that looked about 6'1 brown skin with a little weight on him and a fat face. Then came right back in and did the same thing until he found Quies.

Snatching Quies up off the floor the officer talked shit all the way out the door. "Here get in there with your homie boy" The sheriff said as he cut the zippy ties of his wrist and legs. Quies walked in and walked over to the sink and toilet, to run water in his eyes. He sat down on the opposite of the room. They sat there in complete silence for a moment, and then the guy begins to talk to Quies.

"Hey man the name Trill homie"

"That's what's up, mine Quies"

"Say homie so ...... so...... so where you from" Trill Stutterly spoke

"I'm from Atlanta"

"Ok you 3 hours from me, I'm from Albany"

"Ok that's what's up I know a few niggas from 229"

"Oh yea, who you know from that 9?" Trill asked

"Shid my nigga Gregg, Monyee and my home girl Synephria and Enla B"

I know a few more but that's just off the top"

"Aye Gregg go by "G" don't he?"

"Yea, that's him that's my nigga, cool as a fan"

Quies and Trill chopped it up until the officer came back and got them both. Trill was way in Colorado for some chick that he met off of P.O.F. And got locked up for smoking spic and drinking, they just made him sleep it off. The chick that flew him out there was a lawyer and she was plugged in with all of the judges and DA's. The officer took them and a few other guys back down to intake to be released.

This was the fastest Quies had ever been released from jail. As he walked out the main door he scans the area to see where Punkin and Kim was. Not spotting them right off hand Quies took a seat on the little bench then pulled out his phone to call. as he rised his head up from dialing the number, Kim was blowing the horn as she drove up. Quies stood up and begun to walk towards the car and heard a loud "Boi I see ya, you got two of em" Quies turned around and it was Trill walking with his little lawyer chick.

Quies just smiled and told him to hit him up as he got in the car. The lawyer click that he had caught was fine as hell. She was mix with Asian + Hawaii, and had a nice body from what Quies could tell. That made him think about his hoes and if they where working while he was locked up. As Kim drove off Quies popped the question. "Have the hoes been working?"

"Umm......... yes but not for the full night" Punkin told him

"What you mean not for the full night? What kind of games yall playing?"

"Quies they where only able to work for a few hours, around 11 o'clock the police gave been patrol like crazy for some reason."

"Ok well we gone relocate and slang pussy out of the hotel"

As they arrived at the house Kim and Punkin let Quies walk in to the house first. As soon as he walked Peaches was standing there with an all while Robe and a glass of champagne. "Here you go daddy slip this and put this on" Peaches stated

Quies grabbled the glass and downed the whole thing then got undress and put the Robe on. Kim and Punkin started laughing because they couldn't believe that Quies got naked just like that. Once he had the Bobe on star came and took him by the hand and guided him to the bathroom. Everywhere Quies looked it was Rose pedals and candles. The tub was filled bubbles and Rose pedals. Star slowly pulled off his Robe then helped him the tub. As Quies got settled in, Star turned on some slow music to set the mood. Pebbles came in with a tray of fruit and cheese square.

Red and La La came in behind Pebbles and started massaging Quies as Pebbles fed him. Bunny, Precious strawberry slowly danced their way into the bathroom to put on a show for him. Quies got real relaxed and aroused at the same time. But the girls didn't notice it because of all the bubbles. He called Bunny over and made her get in the tub with him. Quies wanted to finish what he started back at the hotel. He made Bunny sit in his lap and he grabbed her by her things. Bouncing her up and down, Bunny begun moving and squeezing his hand indicating that it was feeling good Quies stood up and bent Bunny over making her grip the rim of the tub.

Not taking it easy at all, Quies pounded her Kitty good and hard. Not being able to handle them good hard and deep strokes, Bunny moaned out stop as she tried to move. But Quies had done wrapped her up with his arms and begin riding her even harder. He made sure she couldn't get away from his custody. Her titter swung back and forth with each stroke. Bunny let out short screams mixed with soft moans. She finally got the strength to take her hand and push Quies back.

When she did that he knew something wasn't right. He pulled out and turned her around, to see two small tears roll down her face.

All the other girls were dying to be next. They liked how he was doing her; they were getting wet just by watching.

"You alight shawty?"

"Yeah, I'm good daddy but I can't handle it like that"

"Ok well say no mo. I'll catch you later when you earn the dick"

"I'm sorry daddy"

Quies didn't even say nothing else to her he just got out the tub. As he walked in to the bedroom he called Kim and Punkin into the room.

"Yea, baby!" Kim answered

"What's wrong boo?" Punkin asked

Quies stood there soaking wet with an hard on," man yall know what time it is, I don't have time for another disappointed Punkin and Kim both smiled as they ran the girls out the room. And before Kim shut the bedroom door Quies shouted out

"Ya'll hoes better be ready tonight" then Kim shut the door.

It was like Punkin and Kim had been waiting on this, because they wasted no time getting undressed. Punkin stop what she was doing and ran to the bathroom to get a wet rag, then cleaned Quies off and said "Now we are ready" and pushed him on the bed. Punkin climbs on top of him an eased her way on his manhood. She went up and down then turned around on it, so her ass would be facing him. Quies smacked her on he ass and she started bouncing harder making her ass clap.

Watching that juicy ass clip made Quies even hoover. He made Kim sit on his face just to join her in before he get in his grove. He made Kim and Punkin both get up and arrange them, so he could take care of them both at the same time.

CHAPTER 8

Later that night Quies was fully energized and ready to make some money. He got dressed and grabbed his pistol, then crept out the room while Kim and Punkin stayed sleep. He grabbed his track phone and they keys to the van off the table. He went a woke up all the girls and told them to get dress and meet he in the van. They slowly came out one after another, and loaded up the van.

"I hope yall don't mind fucking in the same room with each other" Quies stated as everybody got comfortable.

As they drove down road Quies checked his rear view mirror, because noticed a car in and out of traffic behind him. He didn't get a bad feeling like usual. But it was just the thought of him beating up Ice and his crew or whoever they were to him. so he pulled over into the gas station that was down the street from the hotel. The car passed right by them with the police on their tail. Quies let out a small laugh as he parked the car and got out.

He went inside and grabbed a few condoms, two red bulls, wet wipes and some gum for the girls. Quies looked at the young cat behind the glass and told him

"Aye when you get off bring a few of your friends to the hotel down the street, I got some grade a females but ya'll money got to be right." The guy eyes got bucked because he couldn't believe Quies just told him out loud like that. Quies tossed the guy a card and $20 to pay for his things then walked out the door.

But before he could make it out the door a older dude stopped him. Now this guy looked like he could be the police and on the other hand, he looked like an old horny truck driver. “Aye sir doesn't mean to bother you but you did say you had some grade a girl's right?” The older guy asked

“Aye dad you aint the folks are you?”

“Umm ...... can we step over here?”

“Man look I aint got no girls and we aint got nothing to talk about.”

“No! No wait look I'm FBI but I just like to get my rocks off just like the next man.”

“Aye man I fell ya but I don't know what you talking about, I wish you luck” Quies said as he walked off.

The older guy stood there and watched Quies get inside the van and drive off. Not knowing if the man really wanted to spend some money or not, once he told Quies that he was FBI that had done it. Arriving at the hotel Quies parked so he could see the road and monitor the rooms at the same time, before he got out, he passed out packs of gum and told the girls that the wet wipes will be in the rooms.

He made the girls hold up one time before they got out. He had to go get two more room and to let Mr. Faygo know what he was about to do. Mr. Faygo was cool with it because he liked how Quies handle business. And on top of that Mr. Fygo loved watching the pretty girls walk around half naked. Quies rand back to the van after checking out the rooms.

“Aye Bunny and La-La go to the front desk and handle that business with Mr. Faygo”

“Aww daddy can I go take care of Mr. Faygo” strawberry cried

“Nah nothing this time baby everybody has to get a chance”

Bunny and La-La got out the van to handle business like daddy told them too. Then he told everybody else to get out and hit the new strip. Stopping Peaches and Red before they got too far from the van, Quies let them know that they were coming to the room with him. he gave them the key and told them to go first as he locked up the van, and took a good look at the strip. Everything looked good for now, Quies shot back to the room.

"Aye yall know what yall here for right?"

"Yes" they both answered

"Okay before we get started tell me what yall names are again"

"I'm Krystal aka Peaches"

"And I'm Brittany aka Red from meme phis"

"Oh ok and Peaches where you from agan"

"I'm from Los Angeles daddy"

Peaches was Tannish brown long skill jet black hair, brown eyes, 42 inch ass with no stomach, nice juicy breast that fit her body and stood at 5'7. (Sexy ass Latino). Red has a Dirty Red skin tone, with big juicy pink lips, brown hair with blond high lights, she was 5'5 and built like Nikki Ma, Quies looked at both of them ad thought to himself "Damn this is a lot of ass I got to handle." He got undress and made them do the same.

"Umm……. Daddy who you want first?" Red asked hoping he'd say her.

"Shid I want you both" Quies said as he broke the seal on the condom box.

With that entire ass Quies wanted to start off from the back with both of them. Palcing those on the edge of the bed, Quies Rubbed their ass then gave them a smack. Peaches let out a sexy little moan and Red moaned out yes daddy. Quies grabbed his wood and rubbed it up and down Red's pussy. Then slowly went inside of her taking long deep strokes. Quies leans over while still hitting Red from behind, and started kissing and licking Peaches on the ass. He spreader her ass and spitted on to her ass hole, then slowly worked his thumb in and out.

Then he pulled it out and grabbed Red by her hips and begins jerking her back and forth. "Ooh daddy gets this pussy!" Red moans as she threw it back. Quies pushed her in the back to make her ass rise up, and then started stroking her at an angle. Red begun biting on the pillow then put her head under it. Quies went faster and harder, they felt a strong pressure hitting up against his body. Her juices ran down his leg, Quies pulled out and smacked her on the ass, before he went up inside of Peaches.

He gripped Peaches by the hair and pulled her back with each pump. And used the other hand to grip her ass and smack it all in one motion. Quies lift up one of his legs and placed it on the bed, to give him more leverage. Peaches started speaking Spanish with soft moans. Quies didn't understand anything but popi and he knew that was good. He climbed up on the bed with his other leg and made Peaches; put a deeper arch in her back as he plunged down inside of her.

While he jabbed her inside she got welter and creamed all on the shaft of his manhood. Quies continued to drop that dick off in her, while making Red lay on her back with her legs up. Pulling out he climbed down then gave Peaches a smack on the ass spreading her cheeks he kissed and licked her kitty. Then went over to Red and made Peaches get in the same position.

Meanwhile the other hoes were getting it in and time was flying. Kim and Punkin finally woke up and noticed that everybody was gone. They jumped up and head straight for the track.

Back at the hotel the girls started wondering what was going on, because Quies hasn't been in the van all night. they knew Peaches and Red went with him earlier but they didn't know if they were still with him. And each room was paired up for two girls each room. They heard sounds coming from the room, but they just thought it was each other. They all went in the room and went to the side door and knocked on it.

"Yeah who that?!"

"Daddy is that you? It's the girls"

Quies stopped in mid stroked and opened the door.

All the girls looked passed him to look in the room. They saw Peaches and Red in a position they never saw before. Then they looked back at Quies and said

"Daddy you have been in here for hours and we need you out there"

"Ok here I come give me two minutes"

"And here is what we made so far" Star said.

Quies looked at Star then told her "thanks for taking control of then money" Star smiled because she knew he liked that. And when he realized it he still had three move hoes that he hadn't broke in yet. But he was having so much fun with Peaches and Red to the point that he forgot about everybody else. They were the freakiest and that turned him a lot. He took the money told them that he would be right out.

Before he closed the door Strawberry bent down and kissed his swollen manhood. "I'm sorry daddy I just couldn't help it" she stated. Quies shook his head hurried back to the bed, pulling the rubber off them went straight inside Red mouth. They took turns and before you knew it Quies was exploding all over their faces. He grabbed a few wet wipes and cleaned up, then got dressed. As he walked out the room door, he popped the top on one of the Red bulls.

He hurried to the van and put the money in the glove department and sat back. Soon as he got comfortable Kim and Punkin was pulling up. All he did was say "Just in time." He knew if they would have caught him in the room with them two hoes, they would have swore up and down that's all he came to do was to fuck them hoes. Quies sat back and let them pull up next to him. And the first thing Punkin did was lend over to look in the usn, Checking for hoes.

Quies just laughed has he kept his eyes on his hoes. Punkin and kim got out the car and climbed in the uan.

"Damn you was just gone leave us sleep." Punkin said as she Mashed Quies in the back of the head. He just cut his eyes at her with that bitch stop playing look, and Punkin sat back in the set.

"Aye Bae why did you leave the track?" Kim asked

"I thought yall said it was hot over there" Quies replied.

"Oh yea that's right because around this time police would be riding thought."

"Ok cool I'm glad to know that so now I can look for anything out of the ordinary."

"Ok baby not to Jump topic but me and Kim have been talk and we came up with some name for our babies" Punkin stated.

Quies shook his head and chuckled because out of all times Punkin went to talk about baby names.

"Go a head run them by me" Quies said as he continued watching his money. And the more they talked the faster time flew by. Quies jumped out the van to collect his the money from the girls because they'd been booming. He got back in the van and pulled out his Gucci money pouch.

He had everything over to Punkin and told them to go straight home. He could tell that they were getting sleepy. As they were driving off Mr. Faygo came to the window and signal for Quics to come here. Quies looked at him with a puzzled look but quickly walked over to the office.

"Aye my friend young Pimpin" Mr. Faygo called.

"What's good Mr. Faygo, you want two more hoes?" Quies asked.

"No I heard over my police scanner that they were on the way."

"Oh shit thanks for the tip."

Quies ran back to the man and hit the hazard light on. He stood there and waited for his hoes to pulk up. Everyone that was on the strip or just got back came Rushing to the van. Quies advised them to go to a room and to stay there to he said so. He counted the girls as they quickly went to the room. They all was there but two, Strawberry and Bunny was the only two still trying to get that last dollar. Quies kept watch on the streets looking for them and the cops. Until he spotted Strawberry running up the street with some chick.

"I'm sorry I'm late daddy" Strawberry said.

"No time to talk go to the room" Quies replied

"Yes daddy."

"Strawberry ran to the room with the little chick right behind. Quies ready didn't have time to check her about the chick because wanted everybody off the street first. As he turned back around to check the road one more time before he went in the hotel himself on cop car drove. He looked back at the hotel to make sure wasn't nobody out. His heart was beating fast because Strawberry had just left his present. He did need to get locked back up for the same thing go fast.

Quies jumped in the uan to move it in front of his rooms door. As he got out the uan he saw Bunny walking towards him and a guy walking to his car. And if Quies wasn't mistaking it was the same older guy from the gas station. Quies just looked puzzled them told Bunny to go to the room. Following right behind her he couldn't stop thinking that the old mad had done set him up. Quies told all the girls to fleshing up, because it was going to be a minute before they could leave.

He sat back on the bed and turned on TV. Flipping through the channels he thought about CNN news. He wanted to see if anything new popped up on his case. But they were talking about Tump said that he wanted to run for president. Quies called Kim and to her that they would be hone in the morning or later, because it was hot right now and he didn't want to get caught out. The girls always kept them a little Goodle bag with a change of clothes in it.

One by one as they cleaned up they all tried to squeeze in the bed with Quies. It wasn't enough room so he told them to just sprit up and he would take turns each bed. Quies started up a little game just to pass time, and once they got tired of playing they just talked until they all fell asleep. It takes a lot to sale pussy, its hard work because no one wants a lazy fuck. And they been fucking all night so you know they were tired.

CHAPTER 9

Two months in and Quies had done made a name for himself. And him and Mr. Faygo had done became the best of friends. Quies trapped the hoes out of the hotel and that brung customer from all over. He even had other pimps hoes try to get him to pmmp them. The girls had done steped their game all the way up. They was in to role play and everything. But if a trick wanted them to role play it coasted 500 at the door and a extra 100 per hour.

Mr. Faygo let Quies in on a little secrete, on why the police could near come on his property. And if they was even to step foot on his property they would have to pay. That's why guys would get locked up once they left his property if they were dirty. Mr. Faygo schooled Quies on some good shit. Quies was really beginning to see what it was like to live the good life. All of his hoes was getting along and Strawberry just kept bring new hoes to the track for Quies to pimp. He really didn't know how that got started until he thought about it.

It all started with skittles that night, he had to run all the hoes off the strip and she came trailing behind strawberry. Now skittles has put in a lot of work. And still keep her hair died like the rainbow. The little Asian had swa flavor that's swag and flavor, thats why she fitted is so easy. But the other new hoes was just little nat nats. Qures made them best their feet all night. He had done went from 8 hoes to 16. And he treated the all equal when they went out.

And just so happen today was a spoiling day. He took them out to eat at Denny's for Breakfast, then they did the usual hit the mall to shop. Quies let Punkin and Kim handle that head ache, while he promoted the girls as usual. Lunch time rolled around and quies couldn't make up his mind, if he wanted to eat at the mall or take everybody out to a nicer place. Everything got real quiet and just like the movies, a lady screamed out "gun!"

Quies looked down and patted his hip thinking that he had done dropped his pistol. But one he lifted his head back up he seen a group of guys. They were dressed in all back with different clown mask on. Is eyes got buck because he couldn't believe that he was about in a massager. Quies told the girls to run and to try to make it back to the Jans. They all took off running and bullets started flying. Quies tried to give the girl a head start so it wouldn't look like he was leaving them. But shit got real fast and that little table he was hiding behind, wasn't doing no good for him.

Qures jumped up and started running he passed by everybody. And all he called hear was "Daddy wait" and Gun fire. He didn't even look back, all of the scramming from people getting hit and scared of being hit made him not even want to slow down. Until he heard Kim's voice. Quies looked back and seen her on the "Damn white girls always falling" Quies said to himself. Trying to make up his mind if he was going to help her up or leave her, was racing through his mind.

But he knew he couldn't leave his baby Moma stuck like that. Qures ran back to help Kim out and soon as she got off the ground, a guy came over a bull horn and spoke. "Kimberly Allen come out! Come out where every you are" Quies dropped his head because he knew it was going to talk a miracle to get out of this one. As they started running could hear someone from a distance shout out there she is." And bullets came a flying in his direction.

Trying to zig zig with Kim and not get hit wasn't working. Quies took the Desert Eagle off his hip and told Kim to run. Knowing that his gun power wasn't good enough, he just wanted to lay down some cover fire. Kim took off her heels and started running. Quies went one way and she went the other. Taking the attention off of Kim and putting on his self.

Quies slid behind a Kiosk and returned fire. Keeping the heat focused on him. He sat there for a minute trying to think of a way out, until he notice the cart had wheels. He removed the little thing they were using for breaks, and started rolling the cart. As the cart build up momentum to keep. Rolling, the cart. As the cart build up momentum to keep rolling, Quies let it go after firing a few shots from behind it. He took off running and jumped behind this huge flower pot. Sticking the gun over the top and let out two, Quies knew it was life or death from that moment on. He had done ran out of bullets and these niggas was still shooting.

Quies put his gun back on his hip and sat there until he could think of something creative. But it didn't take long, Quics was more happier to see the police then anything. That was the first time a black man was happy to see the police on his side. Whoever those guys was they wasn't backing down. They weren't like the first crew Ice send at the track that night, these niggas meant business. They went shot for shot with the police. Quies slid out the broken window and haoled ass. Didn't look back not once, he didn't care who killed who he just wanted out.

As he made his way to the parking lot he called Punkin to come pick him up. She was already out there but just couldn't come no closer. The police cars were everywhere, blocking off every possible entrance there was Qures finally made to the van and hopped in. Wasting no time Punkin drove off so she could meet back up with

Kim and the other girls. As they got closer Punkim called Kim and told her to head to the house.

"Baby you just done been though hell seen we met." Punkin stated

"Yeah who you telling, I'm about ready to kill yall myself" Joked Qures.

"Bae that wasn't nice at all."

"Don't get all soft on me now."

Punkinn just rolled her eyes at Quies because she fell as if he played at the wrong times. Arriving back at the house, Kim made her was over to Quies to apologize. But Quies didn't feel like talking he was just glad that everybody made it out safe. As everybody walked around the house trying on clothes and putting them up, Quies went to reload the Desert Eagle. Once he was done he laid across the bed. Watch over all of these females was exhausting. Quies jumped off the bed and hit the shower.

Fifteen minutes in Quies heard Kim calling his name as she enter the shower. Quies finished the soap out his eyes and turn around Kim was on her knees telling Quies to come here. Quies walked slow as he rubbed on his self getting primed up. Kim moved his hand and grabbed his meat and put it her mouth. Bobbing her head back and forth until Quies was fully erected. He lifted her up and pinned her against the shower wall. Taking one leg and lifted it up in his arm, white he rammed himself up inside of her.

Quies kissed and choked Kim while he stroked her insides. Making her feel his pain from today. He let he neck go and grabbed her other leg and lifted it up. Bouncing her up and down, Quies eased her down on the bench in the shower. And started fucking her hard, with no remorse. Kim moaned and tighten up around

Quies with each stroke he took, Going deep and hard, Quies felt Kim getting wetter and wetter. He pulled out and flipped her over making her touch her toes.

Quies wrapped his hands around her hips and pulled her back with each Pump. Smacking her on the ass as he felt him self about to climax. He snatch himself out and pot it in Kim's mouth. She topped him off and Quies cam all on her face, then turned around and finish bathing. Once he finish he let Kim wash up and they got out the shower. Smacking her on the ass Quies told her to got dress.

20 minutes later Quies calls a meeting in the living room. He make sure everyone was ok and to let them know that they taking the day off. As he went on, the front door open. Qures stop talking and everybody to be quiet. He looked at Kim like "What the fuck!" Then slowly peaked around the corner but didn't see one. Then He heard a man's voice call for Kim.

"Kimberly honey, It's me daddy!"

Quies didn't let her say anything because he wasn't sure what was going on. You could hear Kim's cell phone ringing form up stairs. She broke away from Quies and stepped into the hallway and called her father. As her father came around Kim took off running and screaming "Daddy!" Punkin walked out to met her dad, while Quies stayed in the living room. Quies wasn't really feeling meeting her dad or mom because of the way they acted when she told them she was pregnant. They all came back to the living room and Quies eyes got back and his mouth dropped.

Kim's dad flipped when he saw all of those people In the have. But once he saw Quies sitting in the corner, he did the same thing. His eyes got buck and his mouth dropped. He had bean dealing with Quies for a while now, and when he realized that all the people was the same hoes that he had been sleeping with. He pulled Kim to the side and asked her what was going on. Kim politely told her dad everything that she had going on in the house.

And in the mist of them talking, Quies walked up to be nosey. Mr. Allen eyed Ques because he didn't like the fact that he had his baby girl pregnant. Quies walked behind Kim and draped his arms around her waist. And put his head on her shoolder and gave her a little kiss on the neck. He could see the steam coming from Mr. Allen's head.

"So what brings you over Mr. Allen?" Quies asked

"Well if you must know I came to tell my baby girl that she need to leave town again until we get things handle."

"Umm....And what things that might be?"

"Don't sit there and act you don't know what's good on. She just told me you all just left the mall."

"Oh yea well in that case I know exactly what's going on."

"Uh Quies how do you know my dad" Kim interrupted

"Oh we bumped in to each other at the gas station that's all" Quies replied.

Mr. Allen started back talking about how Isaac A.K.A Ice was back in the County Jail. Qures busted out saying "Yeah we got to hitting because he was talking about my baby, and had his little group all around him." Kim came from under Quies arms just looked at her and told that it wasn't a big deal, because he handles it. Mr. Allen told Kim that she needed to go back to Atlanta just until they send him back up the Road. Quies could do nothing but shake his head. He ran from Atlanta to get away from some shit and now he has to from Colorado because of his girl.

"Say Mr. Allen how long to we have before we have to leave?" Quies ask

"Well I wish yall would leave tonight" Mr. Allen responded

"Ok look just give me a day or two and we will be gone."

"Thanks for protecting my baby"

"Well our baby now"

Quies walked off trying to think to himself, trying to remember that little operation Ice was talking about in the county jail before they got to fighting. Time passed and Quies was anxiously waiting for morning time to come. He was ready to do his investigation slash steak out. This was about the normal time he would go to do his steak out, but he wasn't familiar with Colorado just yet.

Quies jumped out of bed to go get a glass of Kool-aid just to help him think. As he walked by the living room he saw Mr. Allen in there trying to get laid. He snuck up on them and stood in the door way. Quies saw lady bug turn he down twice before he said some. Lady bug jump off her twin bed and ran over to Quies.

"Daddy I ain't do nothing I swear" Lady bug cried out.

"I know it was all Mr. Allen, you can go lay back down"

"Qures called Mr. Allen to the kitchen and put the press down on him. He hit him with all kind of stuff to make him feel guilty and so he could black mail him at the same time. Now Lady bug was real hoe, because she would fuck for anything before she got with Quies. And what we call that in the pimp game was "Ho drunk", having qualities of a born out hoe. And what Quies was about to do was called "Double Breasted."

That's when a pimp has double duty's such drug dealing or thief. Quies told Mr. Allen that he needed a dirty assault rifle and a FBI vest.

Mr. Allen tried his hardest to buck and say no but once Quies told him what it was for he was all gain. Quies looked at Lady bug them looked at Mr. Allen and said "You like that balck pussy don't you." Mr Allen just smiled and shook his head yes. But Quies being to wonder where was Mrs. Allen, because last time Kim talked to them they was together. So Quies asked where she was, and to come to find out she was in Atlanta working on a case. Quies heart dropped as he went on listening to Mr. Allen. Letting Aim finish Quies could only say "Damn" then changed the topic.

He wanted to make sure Mr. Allen didn't catch no sign and was gong to have everything he had asked for. He double checked with Mr. Allen before walking off. Quies made it back to room with Punknt and Kim and climbed in bed. Feeling more relaxed about his plans, it didn't take him know time to fall asleep.

CHAPTER 10

"Aye man the boss men gone be really upset with how yall running his operation" Ques stated as he walked into Auto body shop. Everyone turned and looked at Quies.

"And who might you be" one of the three guys asked

"Oh I'm Webster Kill them dead" Quies replied

"What kind of name is that?" And what are you talking about"

"Well Ice send me over to see how everything was going and to make sure all of his money and product was it supposed to be."

"Man nigga this is an auto body shop, all we do here is fix cars. So you and your little fancy suit can get out of here unless you got a car for me to fix."

"Oh well hold that thought this should be him calling me right now" Quies said as he reached into his pocket.

"Quies had done set his phone to go off every 30 to 45 minutes, to pretend as if he was really talking to Ice. He walks back and forth playing his role as if he really knew Ice. And each time he would walk in front of the three guys, he would blurt out Key things that only them and Ice knew about Quies hung up the phone and placed it back inside his Jacket pocket. Then walked over and picked his briefcase that had a MP5K submachine gun built inside of it. The FNH was in a holster on his shatter that was conceal by his suit jacket. Once they saw Quies talking to Ice, well what they thought was Ice. They brought Quies inside the office and show him everything.

They pulled out all of the money that was in the safe and sat it on the table. Then brought forth a money machine and started running through it and sat in a gym bag as they were finish. Once all the money was counted up, Quies asked for the drugs. Trying to hit him for everything they had the leave them for dead. As Fruit and Smoke wlaked off to go get what Quies aked for two cars pulled up. But Quies kept it cool and started talking about street shit to make Tone Lo feel even more comfortable with him.

But keep his eyes on Fruit and smoke the whole time. While Fruit and Smoke stop to talk to the guys that just pulled up. As they pushed off to go get the drugs, the other two guys started walking to the office and Quies alarm went off on the phone again. He picked up the phone and moved closer to his briefcase while faking his phone call. The guys walked in and Quies kept his back to them. Trying not to let to many people see his face. Kept talking as he was really on the phone. One of the guys kind of walked to the side, acting like he was getting something form behind the desk just to get a glance at Quies face.

The guy walked out the room pulling his partner with him. As the door shot Quies turned around and started back talking to Tone Lo.

"Yeah that was my other client that want me to hide money'

"So what is it exactly that you do with all this money and dope?"

"Well the money I clean it up with stocks and bonds and the drugs, I just trade out for other things that he might need or want."

"Oh you good."

"Well I try my best and you know I'm from the hood to so I know how the back darkest works. Everybody wants deals or need plugs on things they can't get themselves."

"Yeah you right."

As they chopped it up for two more seconds the door bust open and the phone Rung all at the same time. Tone Lo asked D-Rock and Cash what the hell was wrong with them for busting into his door like that. But before they could explain, Tone Lo picked up the phone and waved at them to be quiet.

THE PHONE CALL

"Aye this Ice how is everything going?"

"Everything is right on time and we are just about finished with your account"

"Ok good, well make sure everything get delivered and keep them ass holes in line."

"Will do boss"

Aye want just a minute, what accountant are you talking about. I ain't hire no damn accountant that what I got you there for."

"So you didn't send nobody over to clean up the money and stuff

"Hell now! Yall better tighten the fuck up and get my shit right or al yall asses going on the choppen block."

Ice hung the phone up and Tone Lo's face. But it was too late; Quies had done already made back to his briefcase, before Tone could even say a word. Quies had the briefcase aimed at him and signal for him to step in front of D-rock and Cash.

"You really want me to move out the way for a briefcase? What you gone do paper me to dead or better yot throw pens at me?"

"Try me and we will see who will get the last write off."

"Oh we got a smart ass on our hands, Get them yall"

Before they could even attempt to make a move Quies opened fire. Tone Lo dove on the ground and D-Rock and Cash ran back out the door. Quies waved the briefcase around sending bullets flying everywhere, just to give him time to pick up the gym bag full of money. He lend to the side, so he could peep out the door. He could see nobody but Tone Lo on the ground bleeding, from the shots he caught in the legs. Quies grabbed a chair and rolled it out the door.

Bullets came flying in but not from the door way. They came from the side of the office. Quies hit the floor and army crawled out the door. Bullet holes was everywhere in the little tin building. And you could hear police sirens from a distance, and Quies knew he had to make a move and make it quick. Looking around for a way out but not spotting it at the time. Until it hit him "Use a car." Quies staied law as he made his way to the cars, that were being worked on.

As he looked for the keys he heard Tone Lo screaming "Over here!" Quies found an all black G wagon with 30 inch Asanti on it. As bad as he wanted the ride for himself, he knew now wasn't the time. Quies started the G-Wagon and looked around for a brick to put on the gas peel! He picked up a can of paint instead of the brick and used a small pipe iron to hold it down. The RPM went up and Quies knock the car out of gear. Screehing tires was all you heard, as the car drove off bearly missing Tone Lo.

Quies picked up the bag of money and the MPSK briefcase and went out the side door. While D-dock, Cash and the other two guys shot up the G-wagon. Quies made it back it his stolen car and dropped the money off. The sirens sound was getting closer and Quies just remember that the other two guys had went to get the drugs. He looked back at the streets then looked at the shop. He knew the drugs had to be close by. He started up the Mercedes-Benz 565 AMG, then spraied shots once again with the briefcase.

Sending the whole little crew running for cover. Quies jumped in the Mercedes and b backed his way off the property into the street. As he slapped he car in drive one of the cop cars bumped him from behind. Quies smashed the gas and took off. It was like half of the police came behind him and the other half hit the shop. All Quies cold think above was making bcak to Mr. Faygo's property. He at least wanted to get close enough so he could run if he needed to.

Quies opened up the arm console and grabbed his gloves back out and put them on. Then took some wet wipe he brought along and stated wiping the car down as drove. He let down the window and quickly wiped the door handle, before having to swerve from behind a car just to barely miss a head on crash with an 18 wheeler.

Quies got back in control of the wheel and speeded up. Having a good head started was helping him big time. But Quies knew he had to get of the straight a way before they set up a road block. He called Kim and asked her for direction to get back to the mall. But once he thought about it, he knew he would be better off finding his on way. He put phone back in his pocket then turned up the radio. It was young thug "Cash Talk", that made him sit up in the driver seat and ride hard.

And as soon that went off Jeezy came on. Quies swerved in and out of traffic with the police hot on his trail. Traffic begin to come to a stand still and Quies could see the flashing lights up a head. He made a quick right into a Pawn shop parking lot, and cut across they came out the other entrance. That gave him a little move time to get an even big lead. Hitting the gas Quies opened the Benz all the way. Doing 120 Mph and still had more to go, Quies jumped on the expressway. Then gave it all he had, the Mercedes went up to 180 quick. Quies breezed thought traffic leaving the cops in the wind.

He jumped off the exit and got back on going the opposite direction. Future came across the radio "March Madness" Ques turned the radio up and hauled ass. The boss speaker was sounding off like two 12 inch sub woofs. As Quies came back up the expressway, the police was going down on the other side. Quies came all the way back around and made it to Mr. Faygo hotel. He parked next door at an empty building, then got out the car and quickly ran back to Kim's infinity.

Placing everything in the trunk then hopped in the driver's seat. He took off hat cheap pin strip suit and put it I a bag and put on his true religion Jean and white T. Then put on his Jimmy choose and a fitted cap. As he pulled off the lot his phone rung, he reached over and picked it up out the passenger seat. It was the damn alarm going off again, he turned it off and sat the phone in his lap. And so as he dropped it, it started ringing again. He flipped the phone over to see who it was, it was Punkin.

"Yo what's good baby?"

"Boy where the hell you at?!" Punkin asked

"Shid I'm on the way home, why?"

"Because it's been a shooting and a high speed chase going on."

"Well it ain't me because I'm on the way home."

"Well ok, but it just look like some of your doing."

"Nah bae not this time "Quies chuckled

"Okay just hurry and come home so you want get caught up"

"Alight I'll be home in a minute."

Quies dropped the phone back in his lap and continued heading home. 20 minutes later Qures was pulling up in the drive ways. Kim and Punkin bust out the door and stood there waiting for him to get at the car. Quies grabbed all of his things and walked in the house. All of his hoes was standing there looking at him as he walked straight by them. Making it to the bed room, Quies dropped everything on the side of the bed. Before he could even make his next move Kim and Punkin came in the room.

Kim looked the door while Punkin made her way over to the bed talking shit and rolling her neck and eyes. Kim ran over behind Punkin and added her two cents. Quies just shook his head and laid back on the bed, as they fused at him to their selves.

It's nothing worst then having two pregnant women fusing at you at the same times. Quies grab a pillow and placed it over his head to drown out as much of it as he could. But it was like they just got louder and louder.

Qures jumped up in the most of saying "I know what you want." He grabbed Kim and Punkin both one by one and threw then on the bed. He snatched Punkin's Pants off and lifted Kim's sundress up. Qures got on his knees and began giving Punkin oral sex while playing with Kim's clit. They both tried to buck and keep talking shit but as Quies went back and forth giving them oral and fingering them at the same time, they slowly gave in.

Quies was good and ready now. He stood up and brought Punkin to the edge of the bed Slowly inserting his self-inside her. Her warm and juices gushed ort with each stroke he took. He slowly penetrated her as he grind his hips to go in a circular motion. Quies speeded up then pulled out as she was Cumming then went inside of Kim and did the same thing. Quies went back and forth for hoots making sweet passionate love.

Two houses had done passed and everybody had done reached their climax. Punkin and Kim was stretched out across the bed sleep, while Quies got his things together.

CHAPTER 11

Later that night Mr. Allen arrived back at the crib. Quies had all of their thing ready to go. Me Allen explained to Kim that they had just busted another one of Isacc drug spots. And that should seal the deal with sending him away for a long time. And they also locked up the guys that was running the shop for him, but they were still looking for the swept that was driving the black Meres.

"Yo me Allen what's good" Quiets said as he halted into term.

"Nothing much just bringing baby girl up to date on everything"

"Right, so how that's coming along because we are about to hit the road in a minute."

"Well in a minute."

"Well it's coming just got to tie up loose ends."

"Oh okay well I got something for you before we leave too."

"Oh yea" Mr. Allen said with a big smile on his face.

"Quies loaded up the vans while Kem and her dad finish talking. He was bringing nine of the girls with him and the other wanted to stay.

"Aye daddy can I ask you something" Peaches said.

"Yeah go ahead" Quies replied as he turned around.

"How is in Atlanta I've never been."

"You'll love it that's all I can say and you want wanna leave"

"Are you still gona take care of me?"

"What you mean, Aint I been doing that so far."

"Yeah, so that means its still cool for me to do this right."

Peaches shovel Quies up against the van and unbuckled his

pant. Squatting and pulling out Quies manhood, she begun slowly Jacking him off until he was fully erected. Peaches wrapped her warm wet mouth around his swollen penis and bobbed up and down on it, while jacking him off and massaged his balls. The slopping and moaning sounds that Peaches made while she performed oral made Quies want more. He grasped the hack of her head and started fucking her mouth. Peaches held her mouth and head steady, while she clutched Qures butt cheeks.

Quies then snatched her up and bent her over the tail end of the van. Aggressively unfastening her coach jeans and pulling them down. Quies placed himself inside of her warm tight Kitty. Each pump he took her ass made a clapping sound from the bodies hitting against each other. Quies pulled her up in to ah up right position, with one hand wrapped around her breast and the other on her hip. Stroking her slowly while smooching on her neck, the soft intimate moans simulated Quies even more. Taking hard deep strokes he felt Peaches getting wetter, Quies pulled his man hood out and was cover it thick white cream.

Turning Peaches around and setting her open inside the van, Qures pulled in close adjusted her legs so he could get inside of her. Quies started pending her wet pussy. Peaches moans begin to get louder turning into sexy screams as she tried to hold it in. The pulse of her inside was contracting with each thrust he took. Making her feel as if they were one. Peaches was so wet that her cu juices squirted down the legs.

Quies begun feeling himself about to climax, so he speeded up. Peaches wrapped her arms around his neck and starting kissing on his earlobe, while moaning. Quies closed his eyes and groaned out I'm Cumming. As he ejaculated inside of her, she softly whispered

I love you into his ear. And before Quies knew it he had done told her he loved her too. The pussy had done got too good to him and he let his emotion come out.

That was one of the rules a pimp was to never do. He was only supposed to reward then they did good, but he was always blessing Peaches with the Royal dick on the low. Beside Pukin and Kim she was next in line. Quies hurried and pulled his pants up, then smack Peaches ass while she fastening belt. Quies looked at his G-Shock and realized that they was out there for 40 minutes. Quies walked in the house with Peaches following behind him. As soon as they walked in the house with Peaches following behind him. As soon as they walked in the house Kim and her dad came around the corner.

"Aye Mr. Allen when you are done don't forget to holk at me "Quie stated.

"Oh yeah I almost forgot, what is it that you need Son?"

Me. Allen walked off from Kim and made his way over to Quies. Quies draped his arm around Mr. Allen's neck pulling him as they walked off. Kim was shocked to see her dad getting along with her boyfriend, soon to be baby daddy. She smiled and headed back to the room with Punkin.

"Aye check this me, Allen, I appreciate you coming through for me."

"Yeah well it better be worth it I could lose my job behind this."

Yeah I know but we both want Kim safe right?"

"Bet your bottom dollar I do that's my baby girl."

"Well you got the right man on the job, that's how you ....Never mind."

"That's how I what?"

"Nah I was just saying how you was able to become a graded"

"Well we not gone speak so go soon with all this miss going on it could stress her out."

"Nah she good but I told you I had something for you right."

"That's right".

"Well look go to the move room and take a seat in about to send something your way."

Mr. Allen gave Quies a looked then smiled as Quies just shook his head. Mr. Allen turned around and took off; he wasted no time trying to get to the theater. Quies went into the room with all of his hoes that were staying in Colorado. He called over Lady Bug and Bunny and told them to go down to theater and take care of Mr. Allen. Once they left out the room he told the other seven girls to wait five minutes then go to theater behind them. Quies wanted them to give Mr. Allen the time of his life.

He told them all to be as freaky as they could, making sure it was to the point that he couldn't take no more. They started giggling like little school girls as Quies when into detail on how he wanted them to fuck Mr. Allen. As Punkin and Kim walked around the corner, Quies cleared up his conversation. He acted as if he was telling them to be the best freaky hoes they could be.

"Umm….. Quies where is my dad?" Kim asked

"Oh he went to use the rest room and he said that he didn't mind waiting here with them until their rides came"

"Aww he so sweat, that's my dad always looking out for me"

"Well yall lets take this show on the road" Quies said rushing everybody out the house, trying not to get caught in his lie.

Everybody left the house and loaded up in the vans. Kim and Punkin get in the infinity and waited for Quies to finish talking.

Quies last words to the girls:

If yall every come to Atlanta and still want to get pimped come to Paradise maintenance service. It's I college park off of God by Rd headed into River dale. Matter of fact just comes to phoenix Blud and you will see the vans.

Quice ran to the car while the girls waved good bye to the rest of the girls. Just with in that little time span that they all stayed together, they had done created a strong bond. As they drove off it got really quiet. Quies sat in the back with a puzzled look on his face. He looked around to make sure both vans was following them then turned back around.

"Alight what's wrong now" Quies asked

"We know what you did Quies" Punkin replied

"Umm.... Hum!" Kim co signed

"Man what are yall talking about I aint did nothing"

"Yes you did my dad told me everything" Kim shaded out

"Man what yo dad tell you, cause he lying on me"

"No he aint Quies, cause what happen today had your name all on it" Punkin added.

"What happen today? Fill me in cause I'm lost"

"Quies my dad told me all about the shooting at Ice shop"

"Okay and what that got to do with me. He told me about it too"

"Yeah that's just cause he don't know it was you but you forgot boo-boo me and Kim been riding with your crazy ass" Punkin stated.

"So yall saying that I shot up the shop and took the police on a high speed chase."

"Yeap it was you, Quies you forgot you call me" Kim singled.

"So are you going to keep playing dumb or are you going to tell the truth" Porkin

"Well we do got a long way home, let me steep on" Lagged Quies

"Quies you play to much I'm serious right now"

"yeah cause what are you going to do when lil Punckin and lil Kim gets here "Kim"

"Hold up how you gone say we having two girls" Quies stated teying to change the conversation.

Quies kept the topic off the what he had done did until he fell asleep in the back seat. Once Kim and Purkin realized that he was sleep, they just smile and shooked their heads.

"Quies alaways tried to talk his way out of trouble when it came down to them two.

CHAPTER 12

I am the next morning Quies was waking back up but only this trme Punkin was in the driver seat and they was parked at Kim's house. Quies looked around before he got out the car and started looghing.

"What's so funny to you this morning" Punkin asked

"I was lousing about the first time I came here on a job."

"On you Kim, you were a customer at fist

"Yea I was just a customer until you put him on the Run. So I guess I should thank you huh?" Kim shot back

"Alight yall we aint gone started that mess over attain" Quies stated.

You right we family now playing so I'm sorry for the smart mouth".

"Im sorry to for the cheap shot I took" Punkie Replied.

"Kim do you remember chasing me out the house naked the first time we did it" Quies asked

"Yes" Kim chucked

They got outside the car and quiets started umbadmg while Kim can Punking showed the girls around Quiets made Sure he took all of his things up to the room first, so he could hide it. He didn't want to starts up that topic about him in Colorado again. As the time went on and everybody got steadied, their stomachs started to growl. Quies order a few pizzas and wonder if Kim stall had a few bottles of ADIA. He went to the party and saw that it was a case in a half. He grabbed these bottles and sat them in the freezer.

Then looked in the Refrigerator and noticed that everything in these had to be thrown out. He called La-La and Pebbles to clean out the Refrigerator and everything else that needed to be in the trash, He went to go find Kim and Parking to let them know it was lot of work that had to be done. And also to talk about living arrangement, because they all wasn't going to fit in this one house.

Qules really wanted to split the girls up from Punkin and Kim. He wanted to be able to stay with Kim and Punkin some nights and the girls the other. As they sat down and talked time went by and the pizza had arrived. Quies paid he delivercy man and shot him a nice little lip. He sat the pizzas on the kitchen and told everybody to grabb a cup. Quies quickly went inside the freezer and pulled out the three bottles of liquor. Puring up everybody a class, they made a toast for the new beginning.

It's about 3 pm and they were partying like it was 10 at night. The liquor had done kick in and everybody was feeling good. The kept at least a bottle or tow in the freezer just in case they needed it. The atmosphere had done changed and they were getting loose. Dandling all on each other, Kissing one another. And they all took turns playing with Quies, even Kim and Punkin interacted with the girls. Kim whisper something into Punkin's ear and she grabbed Quies by the hand. As she led him up stairs, they stopped by the Kitchen and grabbed that half of bottle and took up with them.

Punkin undress Quies then pushed him on the bed. She gave him a little strip show, then threw her Panties at his face as she walked over slowly. Quies pulled her in and started Kissing all over her. Her little baby bump was so sexy on her. Quies kissed and rubbed her belly. She pushed him back down and climbed on top of him, She reached under and grasp Quies Meat and placed it inside of her. Punkin was so emotionally aroused that with that with the first two strokes she came. Smile down at ones as she continued going up and down on him.

Kim walked into the room and said "I'm just in time." Punkin and Quies looked at her as she ran to the closet getting undressed. Punkin kept doing what she was doing. Kim made her wasy over to the bed, with her little bag of toys. The first things she pulled out was the hand cuffs. She looked at Quies and told him

"Not to fight it just let it happen." Quies started laughing.

Because he knew Kim had done lost her mind. He let he hand cuff his arm and legs to the bed. Then she pulled out her oils and little whip.

"Aye Punch staraddle his face and make him eat that pregnant cochea"

Punkia laughed at Kim as she straddled over Quies face. Quies didn't hesitate to please his baby mommas, he gave Punkin just what she wanted. Kim oiled him up then gave him a few licks and sucks to make sure he was good hard. Then she climbed on top of him and slowly went up and down. As she got wetter she went faster and begun spanking him with her whip.

"You have been a bad boy Mr. Quies, now it's time for your punishment ladies you can come in now" Kim said as he grind her way to a nut.

Quies moved his head to look at the bedroom and claimed al on the side of his face. The girl walked in the room already naked. Quies couldn't help but think about how he sat Mr. Allen, for the same treatment back in Colorado before they left. Quies knew he was in for but he was ready as best as he could be. Each girl came and did their only little special trick just tease him before they really got to it. Each one of them knew what Quies liked for them to do, when he blessed them with the royal dick. Quies laid there as they had their way with him.

And each time he climaxed, they would get him right back hard. The liquor had them horny as hell. They each took turns or 3 hours straight, Even Kim and Punkin was a part of the party. Punkin left out the Room to orders some Chinese food because she knew after all of that everybody would be hungry and sleepy. Once the food came Punkin went back to the room. Quies called her over and ask her give him another shot of ADIA.

Quies begged and cried for Kim to let him out of them cuffs. Looking at baby being all helpless made her feel sorry for him. She unstuffed his arms and legs one at a time. Soon as New York got done riding him he jumped op. "You know ya'll done fucked up rights him he jumped p. "You know ya'll done fucked up right" Quio stated right before drilling the rest of the liquor. Shaking his head from the rush of the alcohol, Quies was ready to go. The first chick that was next to him he snatched up.

Quies took them one by one and grudge fucked then until he was satisfied. He knew each position that they had, where they couldn't handle the dick. Quies didn't even worry about Kim and Punkin he had something special planned for them. An hour and a half went by and Quies was reach mg Climx. Not being able to handle non another rand, he took off to the bathroom. All he wanted to do was take a good hot bath and relax.

Punkin came in as he was climbing in the tub. She climbing right behind him. "I cant go no more baby"

"I'm not here for that Quies, I just want to chill."

"Ok cool cause yall got down on me today."

"Boy stop playing you know that's every man dream to be in a room full of women by herself."

"Yeah it is but damn yall just took the dick,"

"Ooh poor baby ton couldn't handle all of that pussy huh"

"Oh I handled it but damn next time give me a heads op"

They sat in the tub for a good 30 minute before they got out and dried off. It was about 7:30 and everybody was still walking around Necked. Quies and Punkn was the only two that had put some clothes on. As made to the kitchen the girls was in and out fixing them something to eat. Quies warm up a few slices of pizza to go with his Chinese food. Sitting down in front of the TV quiets looked around and realized that he really did have it made. He was in the house with nothing but bed bitches. Twenty to Thirty minutes later everybody was full and had done passed out.

Quies took Kim and Punkin toe the bedroom then went back down to cover up everybody else before falling to sleep himself.

CHAPTER 13

The next Morning Qures got up feeling rejuvenate but had a slight hang over. He went down stairs and popped the top of a new bottle and took a few slips just to knock the edge off. When just loaded around. It was like a movie how everybody partied the night before and just fell asleep wherever they was. Quier crossed back over a few bodies then went back up stairs.

Walking Kim and Punkin up so they could get started on their day, which was going to be a long one. Quies need then to handle business with girls and the living arrangements. While he took care of some more things. Quies went and jumped fresh in some Robin Jean and Armani shirt, Red bottom shoe and a black a hit to match the outfit, with a gold MK watch. As he walked by PUnkin and Kim the smell of Gucci Guilty lingered in the air. They were loving his look and smell, but that only made them curious of where he was headed.

"Umm….Quies where are you going?" Punking asked

"To handle business why what's up?" Quies replied back

"Because you are looking and smelling mightily good" Kim answered

"Don't I always "Quies joked as he walked out the room

That bastard got a smart mouth don't he girl "Punkin started

As Quies made his way down stairs he started clapping and yelling "Yall hoes get up, it wake up time." He confiscated all of their cover to make sure they wouldn't lay back down once he left out the room. Quies went outside and jumped in the BMW. He started heaving flash backs, the last time he was in this car he had just killed pat and crew. He never told anybody but every now and then he would dream about Angel.

He really hated that he had to kill such a beautiful girl, but knew he couldn't have left no loose ends. Quies snapped out of his little daze and drove off. His first stop was to this old job. Once he arrived back at Paradise Maintenance Service, he saw a lot new faces. Quies walked right by the chick at the front desk. She put the phone down and came from behind the desk.

"U sir were do you think your going"

"Just calm down lil lady I'm looking for shun I work here,"

"How come I ain't never seen you around here."

"I was on vacation and could you all shon for me."

As Quies looked around he bumped in to T-mac.

"What's good bruh hows work been tearting you?" Quies asked

"Man Cuz I've be back and forth from here and Columbus trying to keep from getting hot."

"What you mean trying to keep from getting hot."

"Shild you know after that little incident you, me and VI had to handle some niggas of our own."

"Word! So what needs to take place you know I owe you one."

"Oh shild we good on that but I just like to stey law key."

As they were standing there talking shun came from the back office. Walking between Quies and T-Mac, Shun gave Quies a big ol hug then torned to T-mac and said "Don't you got a job to do." T-Mac just laughed and walked, he was to player to fuss with shun. She use to like him about never dated him or slept with him because of the job. They walked back to her office.

"So Are you go back for good, you know I can really use you around her."

"Well that's what I wanted to talk to you about"

"Oh really! Hold up where my girl at and why she aint with you?"

"Oh she taking care of business but she'll be by here"

Quies ran his business plan and ideas by shown to see if she was willing to help. The way Quies laid it out there for it sound to good. And it wuld be have business for the company. She would not only please women but she could please men too. Shon wanted to see what the chicks looked like before she agreed. Then she asked Quies when was gang to be his first day back. He smiled and said tomorrow if everything go right with our business agreement. He got on the phone and called Punkin and told her to bring the girls by the shop.

But they had done split the girls up, she had some and Kim had the rest. He let it be known that shun wanted to see her and the product, before she agreed to what they talked about. As Quies continued talking to Punkin making sure everything was in please or going was it needed too, he caught Shun staring at him. He removed the phone from his ear and covered the speaker and asked her what was up. She motioned nothing and for him to get back on the phone. Quies hurried and end his phone call, then went back to telling business.

Quies noticed that shun had lust all in her eyes. He wrapped of their little in setting and told her that Punkin would be by later with his hoes.

"So Quies how serious are you and Punkin?"

"Now Shon you know that's your girl…

"What are you talking about I just wanted to know" Said shon cutting him off

"You know we can't be fooling around I see it all in your face."

"Hell I just wanted another Round just to see if you still got it."

"Well holla at Punkin and see if she would set it up."

"Oow that's cold but that's what's up."

As Quies walked out the office shun smacked him on the ass. Quies turned around and Shun was laden on the door licking her lips. As Seky as it was Quies knew he would never hear the end of it, if he would have gave in and gave her some. Quies left the shop and hit the streets. It felt like forever since hed Road around the streets of Atlanta.

MEAN WHILE

Pukin was getting her together when her phone rung.

"Hello" Punkin answered

"What's up girl! So you wasn't gone let me know you whole back in town.

"Girl you know I was gong to tell you, I was trying to surprise but Qules beat me to it"

"Yea I see you still holding on to him, that child no himself"

"Don't he doe, but don't get to excited cause he is mine."

"Girl! I know you aint for regal, all that fuclong he be doing."

"Yeah I know but that's just business his heart is will me."

"Child you are crazy but when you coming over."

"Well we are just about finish over here go I guess in about an hour go.

"Ok well just call me when your on the way"

Punkin hugs up the phone and go back to what she was doing.

If dawn on her that shun was checking Quies out, she knew how Shun operated after all those years of working with her and sleeping with her. She picked up the phone and texted her "Don't even think about it we just got back, but if need to be I'll stop by tonight and wax that ass for old times". Then sat her phone down and went to check on the girls.

ONE ANOTHER NOTE

Kim and her half of the girls were still at Wal-Mart shopping. They were getting so much attention to the point that Kim had to call Quies.

"Yo what up baby?"

"Where you at?"

"I'm in college park handle business why?"

"Because I'm at Wal-Mart and the girls are getting a lot of attention".

"Bae we are back in ATL now you know how niggas act when they see a group of fine women. But tell them to give out paradise maintenance service number and ask for the maintenance women special and that's how they can get at them"

"Oh yea that's right. I will still stuck in Colorado Bae"

"I know ….. but you need to call Punkin."

"Ok baby and when are you coming home?"

"I'll see you when I get there crazy"

As Quies hung up the phone Kim heard him shouting out some guy by the name "Clay-Co." She wonders what he had going on. They walked around one more time to make sure they everything before heading to the check-out line. As they waited in line Kim called Punkin to see what was up.

PUNKIN

Racing to pick up her phone she thought it was Quies calling back, but she noticed that it was only Kim

"What's up girl?"

"Aye Quies told me to call you what's going on?"

"Oh nothing we just got to take the girls over to my old job"

"Okay so your girl Shun is going to help us out?"

"Um I ready don't know what they talked about and hold on for "Second"

Punkin opened a text from Shun that was telling her to come over tonight so she could kiss that pretty pussy of hers. Punkin started laughing as she got back on the phone with Kim. "Girl what's so funny" Kim asked

"Oh I was just reading a text but how much longer are you going to be before you come back to the house?"

"I'm in line now so I'll be there shortly."

"Ok I'll see you when you get here"

Punkin and Kim got off the phone and finished up what they were doing Punkin had the house set up for the entire girl to have their own space. She was better at decorating them Kim.

MEAN WHILE

Quies was just living his old stomping grounds. He had hit star ship to get a few toys, he wasn't going to let Punkin and Kim get away that easy. As he waited for the light to turn green he spotted a rose man. He waved for him to come to the car and bought the entire roses he had at his little stand. The guy loaded up the back seat and Quies drove off. The whole time he was out he kept his ears to the street, trying to see if anybody was talking about what happen.

But it was all old new everybody was talking about all new stuff. And come to find out two of his closest friends had passed. One got gunned down at a gas station and the other fell asleep behind the wheel.

It was like the streets got even worse while he was gone. It had done got late and Kim or Punkin had done called him. He slowed down as he drove by Angel's old place. He reached in the back seat and grabbed two roses threw them on the ground next to the memorial site.

As soon as he drove off, his phone rung and a cop car drove by. Quies heart started beating out his chest. He kept driving trying to play it cool; once he got out of sight he made a right at the light. Quies didn't stop until he got on the express way. He's phone went off again only this time he answered

"Hello"

"Damn bae we haven't talk to you since earlier are you ok?"

"Yea I'm good, where you at?"

"We all are up here at the shop"

"Ok good stay there I'm on the way"

Hanging up the phone he started reflecting to himself. That was a close cause even if they didn't have anything on him. He didn't know the first thing to tell the coop if he had stopped him. He didn't know anybody in this neighborhood, so he could lie and say he just left a friend's house. Quies did eighty all the way to the shop.

Arriving at the shop Quies didn't even bother to go in his stomach was touching his back. He called Punkin back and told her to bring everybody out so they could grab something to.

Quies texted Punkin and told her to go to Atlantic station. As they came out he drove off. Quies wanted to boat them their so he could have everything set up. Twenty minutes later he was pulling up at Fox spot + Grill. He hopped out and went inside to tell the waitress that he needed a area for 13 people. She gave him a little table vibrator and he took back off out the door to park the car. Once he parked the car he grabbed two of the buckets and put all of the Roses in them

As he was making his way back to the restaurant people kept stopping him trying to buy Roses. The table mortar was going off, so he hurried back. As he walked in he saw Peaches, La-La, Strawberry, Punkin was standing there wait to be seated. Everybody else road down to park the car, Quies handled the waitress the mortar back with one single Rose, then told her that it should be nine more women that's with them. As they sat at the sure everybody got a dozen. Shun and Kim walked in with the rest of the girls and got escorted by the waitress.

Kim and Punkin sat on each side of him as they order their food. As they waited for their food Quies asked Shun what was up and did see come up with an idea yet.

"Yea we talked about it at the office for a few hours"

"Damn yall didn't even think about calling me huh?!"

"Yeah but your baby Mommas took care of it for you and they had an little extra to go with your plan to make it sound even better."

"Olc cool so we start tomorrow right"

"That's right and you better not let us down."

As their food come out, Quies see a familiar face but he wasn't just sure if it was her. But the whole time he ate he never took his eyes off of her. Quies looked in his buckets and noticed one was over halfway full. He got up and grabbed the bucket and passed out a single rose to every lady until he got to the one he wanted. When he approached her, he took out the last three Roses and said complimentary of paradise maintenance service, just like he told everybody else.

As she turned around from the bar Quies checked her out. She had long honey blond hair that matched her caramel skin tone, her hazel-green eyes made him want to melt. The fragrance of channel 5 floated in the air. The black strapless dress she had on was hugging her body. It seemed like everything had got quiet around him, the only thing that was moving was the chick's lips. Once she stop talking and stared at Quies he immediately came back too.

"Excuse me what was you just saying"

"Huh same Quies I guess you got lost again in all this fineness"

"Sanaa I thought that was you gives me a hug"

"Quies you are too funny and we got to stop meeting down here like this"

"Damn girl why is it every time I see you, you are breath taking and the time stops"

"Boy hush don't be trying to run no game on me, what are you doing down here"

"Oh we are having a little business meeting" he stated pointing at the table Punkin and Kim noticed that Quies was pointing at the table. While Quies kept talking Kim and Punkin headed his way. He was deep in conversation with sane that he forgot about everybody else.

"Excuse me but you must forgot that you were in a meeting "Punkin said as she realized that she was the same chick from last time.

"Here I come now just give two second"

Punkin rolled her eyes and stood waiting for Quies to walk away with her. Quies looked at her hoping that she would go on back to the table but she didn't budge. Quies grasp Sanaa by the hand and gave it a small little peck.

"Nice seeing you again" Quies stated

"Well seeing you again" Quies stated

"Well maybe next we can actually go out and chill" Sanaa replied

"Don't worry it want be" Punkin said as she pulled Quies off.

Quies looked back smiling as he winked his eye at Sanaa. Once they got back to the table everybody was ready to leave. Quies threw a few hundred on the table to take care of the bill then walked off. When they got to the garage parking lot, Quies realized that Punkin was leaving with Shun. His whole plan went out the window. He jumped in the BMW and headed home.

30 minutes they were arriving at the house, Quies was a little upset because Punkin didn't come home. He didn't even want to be bothered. Quies lay across the bed and thought about Sanaa. He couldn't believe that he kept missing his out on getting up with Sanaa. With Sanaa on his mind he drifted off to sleep.

CHAPTER 14

The next morning Quies wake up to a slupping sound with a warm stroking feeling around his man hood. Quies looked down to see Punkiny sucking him up. He waited for a minute then took his dick at her mouth.

"Huh not this morning you sucked enough pussy last night."

"Oh so you mad now that I went over Shun's house?"

"Nah I just got to get ready for work that's all"

"Quies you ain't shit"

"But you love me tho"

"Quies jumped off the bed and got dress. While he was brushing his teeth he check his cash. Pulling out his gym bag, he looked inside and everything was just the way he left. He had over two hundred thousand that he took from Ice. And he really didn't have to work but he just wanted it to look good. Quies went to wash his mouth out then made sure everybody else was up. They were up and dress waiting on him. Everybody loaded up except Kim, she had over things on her plate.

As they drove off Quies begun to wonder what was it that Kim really did. She never work a day since he known her. While driving down the express Quies spot a blue Monty Carlo just like the one pat drove. The Monty Carlo was gaining on them fast and Quies started

Thinking to him, "Damn I know I killed this nigga." Trying not to panic as the car pulled up beside the van. Quies lend over just enough to see inside the car. It was Pat's mom behind the wheel.

Quies took a deep breathe, as she drove off with a for sale sign in the back window Quies got off at his exit and headed to the shop. Once he arrived at the shop he noticed everybody was crowded at the door going in. "Yea them hoes been fucking all night" Quies said to himself as he parked the van. Punking parked right next to him, Quies gave her a look that would kill then mouthed.

"I'm gone get yo ass."

Punkm looked back at him with a puzzled look and mouthed back "What". Quies didn't even stay nothing he just got out the van and walked in side. As he was headed to the back Punkin called his name. He looked back but kept walking, he knew that would got her to follow him. Qures load up his van and heard Punkin call his name, while she walked to the back of the van where he was at. He had done got primed up waiting for her to get to the back up the van.

Soon as she came around the open van door, Quies snatched her in the van. He lifted up her Gucci sundress and pulled her panties to the side. Then went inside of her aggressively. As he pound her from the back he being talking to her.

"Who told you to give u my pussy."

"Nobody" Pukin moaned

"You better not do it no more"

"I'm sorry"

"That ain't what I said…I said you better not do it no more"

Quies said as he smacked her on the ass.

"Oh! I want daddy I promise" Pumkin moaned even sexier the before.

"Quies hurried up and caught his nut while Punkin was climaxing. Once they were finish Quies walked Punkin back in shop so he could get his paper work. Punkin bit on her bottom lip all sexy like as she stared at Quies. Shun came out her office and told Quies, that if they were to get any specials today for the girls she would let him take them. Before leaving back out the shop Quies stop by the bathroom to clean up. His first job was a special. He stopped by a gas station and grabbed a breakfast biscuit with two Rellbuls.

Arriving at his job site, he knew it was something up with the house. If felt like he been there before but he wasn't sure cause a lot of houses looked alike in this subdivision. He got out went to the door and ring the doorbell.

As the door open, he saw Sanaa standing there in her Robe.

"How you doing today Ma'am My name is ….."

Sanaa had done cut him off and told him to come on in.

"I bet you didn't think you would see me so soon" Sanaa asked

"Nah I didn't, and especially not like this."

"Yea I know I had to find someway because of your little girlfriend was all in the way last night."

"So damn how was you able to get me as the first job."

"My little secret and the problem is this way."

Sanaa took Qures by the hand and led him up stairs. Once they made in u stairs Sanna let his hand go and told him right this way. Quies let her go a few steps ahead of him so he could watch her ass bounce in the robe as she walked. Sanaa got to her bed room door and dropped her Robe. She strutted across the bedroom floor while Quies stood at the door. She looked back and stuck her finger in her mouth and slowly pulled it out and signal for Quies to come here.

Quies being to make his way over to the bed as Sanaa laid there with her legs up. Quies stop and turned a rand a went back to close the door.

But before he close the door all the way he stuck his head out and said. “Well this is the farthest this story goes you have read enough about my life” then smiled as he shut the door.

THE END